MW00459835

TOOTH
AND
CLAW

By Craig Johnson

The Longmire Series

Also by Craig Johnson

Stand-alone E-stories

CRAIG JOHNSON

TOOTH AND CLAW

VIKING

VIKING
An imprint of Penguin Random House LLC
penguinrandomhouse.com

LIBRARY OF CONGRESS CATALOGING-IN-PUBLICATION DATA

Names: Johnson, Craig, 1961– author.
Title: Tooth and claw / Craig Johnson.
Description: New York: Viking, 2024. | Series: The Longmire series
Identifiers: LCCN 2024014828 (print) | LCCN 2024014829 (ebook) |
ISBN 9780593834169 (hardcover) | ISBN 9780593834176 (ebook)
Subjects: LCGFT: Detective and mystery fiction. | Novels.
Classification: LCC PS3610.O325 T66 2024 (print) |
LCC PS3610.O325 (ebook) | DDC 813/.6—dc23/eng/20240419
LC record available at https://lccn.loc.gov/2024014828
LC ebook record available at https://lccn.loc.gov/2024014829

Printed in the United States of America
1st Printing

For Frank Carlton,
a better fishing buddy you couldn't have.

Who trusted God was love indeed
And love Creation's final law
Tho' Nature, red in tooth and claw
With ravine, shriek'd against his creed

—*"IN MEMORIAM A.H.H.," BY ALFRED,
LORD TENNYSON*

If it's black fight back. If it's brown lay down.
If it's white say goodnight.

—*BEAR ATTACK PROVERB*

ACKNOWLEDGMENTS

Like a lot of people, I'm a serial reader and tend to stumble onto a writer and if duly impressed turn around and buy every book they've ever written. I went through an Alistair MacLean period in my teenage years, grappling through the Scotsman's thrillers such as *The Guns of Navarone, Ice Station Zebra,* and *Where Eagles Dare.* I can't say he was a great writer, but he was great at what he did: fast-paced and macho adventures in exotic locales. Exactly what I was looking for at the time.

I've referred to thrillers as mysteries with lobotomies, but MacLean never fell prey to the you-know-who-it-is-in-the-first-chapter-and-now-have-to-sit-through-five-hundred-pages-of-chase formula. He kept you guessing until the end with characters that couldn't be described as fully fleshed out, but certainly kept you leaping pages like a reindeer.

Personally, I've enjoyed writing novellas over the years, and *Tooth and Claw* was started almost five years ago but then stalled when I wasn't sure how I wanted to tell the tale. Then I remembered trusty MacLean, whose writing style has been described as "Hit 'em with everything but the kitchen sink, then give 'em the sink, and when they raise their head drop the plumber on 'em."

The next problem was the environs for *Tooth and Claw* and how things were likely to get boring if the entirety of the action took place out on the big ice of the Northern Slope of Alaska, which brought back memories of another story.

I first became aware of the legend of the SS *Baychimo* in an attic literary pile of my father's, where I found a July 1938 copy of *The World Wide Magazine* that contained the article "An Arctic Ghost-Ship." The ghostship *Baychimo* has haunted the Arctic for almost a hundred years, looming in and out of the frozen mists. She was last sited in 1969, which was chronologically perfect for my purposes and Walt's. Researching the ship beyond the four-page article proved to be rough sailing, but I finally reaped rewards in Anthony Dalton's *Baychimo: Arctic Ghost Ship*, which provided a great deal of the history cited here.

Heading out with a story and style, I now needed an antagonist for the good sheriff, someone or something the likes of which he'd never faced before.

I fish in Alaska on an annual basis and have had my share of bear encounters, the closest being a surprise meeting with a Kodiak on the banks of the Kanektok River, where I discovered how I'm going to die—talking. Armed with only a 10-weight fly rod, I've never felt as vulnerable as when standing there with that giant bear hovering over me. Fortunately for the writing of this book and others, the guides came running with air horns and the Kodiak reluctantly turned away from his ready-made buffet.

Most bears don't behave like the nanurluk, thank goodness, but as much of a believer as I am in their continued existence, protection, and careful conservation, polars can't be described as particularly cuddly. They're one of the few carnivores and the largest land variety that are known to actively stalk human beings, and given the small amount of interaction they have with people, they simply don't fear us.

I remember talking with an elderly Yupik friend of mine in Anchorage who told me his son had been hired as a spotter for one of the research groups. He went on to explain how when they first land a plane out on the big ice, they immediately set up a shooting tower, and the spotter's job is to climb up there and keep the polar bears from getting in too close, sometimes having to shoot them to keep them from killing and eating members of the party.

I asked him, How, in a completely white environment do you sight-in on an all but white bear?

Pointing to the center of his face, he replied, "You aim for the nose."

Books are like ships, and I wouldn't have much of a chance of avoiding the icebergs if not for all the following.

My marvelous agent, Gail "Sailing Master" Hochman, and her right hand, Marianne "Master-at-Arms" Merola, are steady at the wheel.

Bringing out the big caliber at Viking/Penguin would be Brian "Boatswain" Tart and Jenn "Able Sea Person" Houghton.

Wo-manning the helm would be Sara "Navigator" Delozier and the ever-faithful Magdalena "Deck Cadet" Deniz, Johnathan "Swabby" Lay, and Michael "Oiler" Brown.

To the west with a sharp eye is Christine "Quartermaster" Choi and belowdecks is Alex "Cookie" Cruz-Jimenez and Molly "Gunner" Fessenden.

As always, keeping things shipshape are Eric "Chief Engineer" Wechter and Francesca "Sparky" Drago.

And last but certainly not least is the North Star of celestial bodies and the light touch that steers me through life's reefs no matter how storm-swept the seas, Judy "Captain" Johnson.

Tooth
and
Claw

1

"What was that?"

Henry Standing Bear looked at me and smiled. "My move."

I glanced down at the weathered chess set between us as Lucian Connally stood on the patio of room 32, turning the three T-bones on the outlaw grill he wasn't supposed to have in the Durant Home for Assisted Living. Stretching his back with a hand at its small, the old sheriff took a deep breath and blew out a lungful into the frigid night and announced, "It is a beautiful evening out, and I'm thinking we should dine on the veranda."

He was framed perfectly in the twinkling Christmas lights that surrounded the patio doors, even though it was New Year's Eve and freezing. "It's twelve degrees outside, Lucian."

Dog, sitting on the sofa he wasn't supposed to, watched him stomp off into the cold, which was nothing new in that he watched everything Lucian did concerning raw meat.

New Year's Eve notwithstanding, Tuesday nights were

chess nights at the "old folks' home," as Lucian referred to it, but sometimes our gracious host had other duties and left the board to us lesser masters. I'd used the Bird's Opening, 1.f4, but the Bear hadn't responded with the usual setup, with b3 and Bb2. Instead he fianchettoed his king's bishop for a flagrant d5. "You're going to lose your bishop," I said.

"Perhaps."

My eyes went from the old sheriff and back to the board to study the Cheyenne Nation's move. "Pretty aggressive opening."

"Yes."

Lucian limped back in and eyed the board with me, taking a stance that relieved the pressure on his prosthetic leg as he slipped off his insulated ranch coat and puffed on his pipe—something else he wasn't supposed to be doing inside the facility. "The Polar Bear System."

"The what?"

He nodded his chin toward the board and tossed the coat onto the sofa beside Dog. "It's a mirror image of the Leningrad Dutch defense." Reaching over the table, he picked up the bottle of Pappy Van Winkle's Family Reserve Twenty-Three-Year-Old and poured himself another dram. "Risky stuff; most you can hope for a lot of times is a draw."

The Cheyenne Nation's face remained unreadable. "Sometimes a draw is a victory . . . Especially when dealing with polar bears."

Connally snorted, then sipped his bourbon. "And what the hell do you know about polar bears, Ladies Wear?"

Henry's dark eyes met mine before responding. "Actually, quite a bit."

"You know, there are times when I think—and I say this with the greatest respect and admiration—that you're full of shit." He stared at the Bear for a moment and then freshened both our tumblers. "When were you ever that far north?"

The Bear pointed his lips toward me. "Visiting him."

Lucian sat the bottle down, sipped his bourbon, and studied me. "When you were up on the North Slope?"

I, in turn, studied the board. "Yep."

"You never told me the Injun came up there."

I shrugged and placed a finger on a piece. "It never came up."

"Get your finger off that knight."

I removed the finger and looked at him. "What?"

Lucian held the glass of liquid spirits to his nose, not drinking; the amber light reflecting and illuminating the lower planes of his face in a devilish visage. "My finely honed detecting skills lead me to believe that there is a story here, one that I may have never heard."

The Bear said nothing for a few moments and then reached into his chambray shirt pocket and carefully pulled something out, placing it at the center of the board. It was something wrapped in oiled canvas tied with sinew, with two small wooden beads attached to the ends.

I stared at the relic. "Is that what I think it is?"

He nodded, his face like a carving.

Lucian lowered his tumbler and looked at the item. "What the hell is it?"

Henry took his time answering. "A totem."

"Of what?"

The Cheyenne Nation raised his eyes to mine. "Perhaps . . . An artifact from when we were young. Do you remember that?"

I smiled. "Sometimes, but sometimes it seems like it happened to someone else, like a dream or a movie or a book that I can only remember the good parts." I reached down and touched the thing. "Good to see it; reminds me that it was us and that the story was real."

He held his gaze on me. "*Is* real."

I huffed a laugh and then studied his face, somber as a landslide. "You think the nanurluk is still out there?"

"The what?" Lucian sat his tumbler down and reached out for the packet. "What in the hell are you two talking about?"

"Do not touch it."

The old sheriff paused in a way I'd never seen him, his hand hovering above the small bundle. "Why the hell not? He did."

"He is allowed." The Bear picked up his tumbler and took a small sip, making a face and setting it back on the coaster beside the board. "He was there."

"Where?"

"Nuiqsut."

"And where, pray tell, is that?"

"North Slope, within the Arctic Circle."

Our host, discerning that the story was Henry's to tell, sidled over, sat on the arm of my chair and pointed at his wristwatch. "Well, you've got seven minutes to tell me this story before I have to turn those steaks."

The Bear flicked a glance at him. "This story might take longer than that."

STATION R3, NUIQSUT, NORTH SLOPE, ALASKA

DECEMBER 21, 1970

"What was that?"

Henry looked at me and smiled. "My move."

It was hard to hear him with all the noise that emanated from the rig, a thrumming from the walls along with the other ancillary noises of a small city crammed into what sometimes felt like a steel ice box. "Are you trying to lose this game?"

He ignored my question, glancing around at the metal walls devoid of any decoration. "So, *this* is what you have been doing for the last month?"

I lifted the Cattlemen's Steakhouse mug that I inherited from the previous chief of security from Oklahoma, the one who shot himself. "I've been practicing my drinking too."

He scanned the rest of the cubicle, taking in the fluorescent lights overhead, the two bunk beds where we sat facing each other, and finally the small magnetic chess set that sat on a footlocker between us. "I can see why."

After moving my knight out, I threaded my fingers into my

beard and figured I needed to defend my recent life choices. "It's cold here, and after Vietnam and Johnston Atoll, I thought I needed some cooling off—maybe in more ways than one."

He nodded silently.

Reaching over, I pulled a bottle of J.P. Wiser's Canadian whisky from the crate that served as my nightstand and poured another drink. "The pay is good."

He moved a pawn. "It better be."

Swirling the Canadian rye in the ceramic mug, I shot a look at him over the rim. "Did you just come all the way up here to make me feel worse?"

"I do not think you need any help with that."

I sipped my drink and stared at the chessboard, unfocusing my eyes. "You know, I used to think that Wyoming was the end of the world, but then I came here."

"And why did you, honestly?"

"Maybe a confession of despair concerning the veneer of civilization, or the fact that I wanted to see a voiceless icescape that despises movement and attempts to freeze the blood in your veins—maybe that's all we deserve."

He stared at me.

"I guess I wanted to see it."

He looked around the room again, placing another pawn into immediate peril. "See this?"

I took the pawn. "You *are* trying to lose this game."

He shrugged, finally admitting. "I am only here for seventy-two hours, and I would prefer not all of it be spent in this room."

There was a beep from the intercom system on the wall by the door. I stood and walked over, hitting the broad tab at the bottom of the cream-colored plastic device. "Longmire."

Static. "Chief, we've got a problem."

I depressed the tab again. "I told you, just call me Walt."

Static. "Right, right . . . Well, we've got a problem in the commissary."

"Yep?"

Static. "One of the younger guys has gone a little buggy and grabbed a meat cleaver. He's holed up in the pantry and won't let anybody near him."

"Who?"

Static. "Frazier."

"My Frazier?"

Static. "'Fraid so."

I placed my mug on the chess set and opened the locker that served as my closet, then took out my holstered Colt .45 and put it on before gesturing for Henry to follow me out of the room. "Looks like you get your wish."

Living on an oil rig is something akin to living on a submarine in that the quarters are tight; I'm assuming in an attempt to heat the smallest area possible. As Bear and I charged down the narrow hallways and stairwells, I pulled out the big semiautomatic Colt just to make my priority clear, and the crews that were up and about quickly parted to make way. "Make a hole and make it wide!"

The Bear's voice carried from behind me as we ran along. "Buggy?"

I nodded as we turned a corner and dropped down another stairwell. "Shift workers, mostly. After working nights for a few weeks, some of the guys can't take it and get a little emotional, start seeing and hearing things."

"And this Frazier is one of your security attachments?"

I pushed through a set of double doors that led into the mess hall. "One of my swing shift guys who has been showing a few symptoms."

Catching up with me, Henry continued the conversation as most of the rest of the people in the room were either on their way out or were pressed against the walls. "Besides grabbing a cleaver and threatening the citizenry?"

I nodded. "Yep, he was spotting for one of the geology teams and was complaining about somebody screaming all the time."

"And what was the problem?"

I pulled up short at the other end of the commissary where the kitchen staff and one of the administrators stood, casting worried looks through the portholes in the swinging doors and into the kitchen. "*He* was the one doing the screaming."

Taking a deep breath, I called out. "Hey, what's for dinner?"

Jim Sanderson, the person with whom I'd spoken to on the intercom, turned to me. "Not pizza."

"What's wrong with pizza?"

"Your crazy security guy has all of them in there and doesn't appear to be in a sharing mood."

"What, he's cooking pizzas?"

He gestured toward the porthole window. "See for yourself."

Leaning over the smaller man, I peered through the glass into the kitchen where George Frazier was standing in the middle of the room, holding a cleaver and sucking on a piece of frozen pizza before raising his head and screaming at the ceiling.

Stepping back, I cut a look at Sanderson. "He's eating it raw?"

"The kitchen staff wouldn't cook it for him, so he decided to self-serve."

"Has he been drinking?"

"Hasn't everybody?"

I ignored the remark and stepped by him, holstering my .45 then pushing open the door and entering the kitchen where Frazier stood, an uneven stack of plastic-wrapped pizzas strewn behind him on a stovetop. "You get that delivered?"

He took the pizza out of his mouth. "Fuck you."

I sighed at him, a very large individual with thick glasses and a wild hairstyle that could only be described as a side-swiped Afro. "You're scaring people, George."

"Fuck them too."

"What, because they wouldn't cook you a pizza?"

I stepped toward him, but he raised the cleaver and screamed a long and plaintive cry at the heavens before speaking. "Stay back, big man, or I'll cut one of your arms off."

"George, you can't stand in here and suck on frozen pizza, first of all because it'll take all night for you to eat three slices, and second of all because you're interrupting business as usual and you know that with the company, that's a no-no."

"Fuck the company."

"George, you're not leaving me many options here."

"Sure I am. Turn around and get the hell out." He tilted his head back and screeched at the ceiling again.

"George, you have to stop doing that."

"Doing what?" He stuck the frozen pizza back in his mouth.

I sighed again. "How 'bout I cook your pizza for you?"

"Why?"

"Because I can't stand watching you eat it like that, it's disgusting."

He thought about it. "I want more than one."

"I don't care, George. I'll cook all of them if you want."

He gestured behind me with the cleaver. "Who's that?"

I turned to see Henry, who had slipped through the double doors and now waited, his arms folded. "That's the pizza specialist. We flew him in from Fairbanks."

"He doesn't look like a cook."

"Sure he is."

"Looks like a harpoon chucker."

"He does that on the side." I stepped forward. "Gimme the cleaver, George."

He swung the thing and screamed at the ceiling again before pointing it at Henry. "He cooks the pizza first."

"Sure." I stepped aside as the Bear nodded at me and then moved past, reaching down to turn a knob on the stove beside Frazier, the soft pop of the gas igniting within.

The security man watched Henry work as he took a pizza from the stack and began unwrapping it. "Medium rare or well-done?" As George considered the question, the Cheyenne Nation swung the point of an elbow around, catching him just under the right ear, whereupon he dropped like a poleaxed steer. "We will go with well-done."

Stooping down, I grabbed the cleaver and we picked up the unconscious man, the Bear helping to shrug him onto my shoulder as we walked him out of the kitchen and past the administrator and culinary staff. "I think he's had enough."

Fortunately, I didn't have to carry him far because the security offices were in the same module as the commissary. Our emergency jail cell was a bear cage that had been left by a National Geographic expedition—there weren't any bloodstains in the thing, so I supposed the expedition had been a success.

Rolling Frazier onto a cot, I retreated and then secured the gate with my handcuffs before heading over to my desk to search for a pen and start the paperwork, which would likely have him shipped off the facility and end his security career within the greater petroleum industry.

As I opened and closed drawers, I finally found a BIC pen while Henry sat in the chair on the other side of my desk. "That was diverting."

I snorted as I filled out the top of the incident form. "We like to show visitors a good time." I was about to add more when I noticed Sanderson standing in the doorway. "Can I help you, Jim?"

He nodded. "There's a problem."

I gestured toward the bear cage. "Not anymore."

Sanderson leaned in the open doorway. "Frazier was supposed to be on the security detail for the U.S. Geological Survey that's doing a core testing tomorrow morning."

"Where?"

"Out on the big ice."

I leaned back in my chair. "Why are they core testing sea ice?"

"Worms."

I dropped the pen onto the forms as a form of protest. "Excuse me?"

"Ice worms . . . something about ice worms."

"You've got to be kidding."

"Nope."

I thought about it and then gestured toward the cage again. "He'll sleep it off and be fine in the morning."

Sanderson took a few steps and then placed a hand on the bars. "Chief, I'm not sending a USGS team out with the screaming pizza-sucker."

It was quiet in the room, except for the numerous and sundry noises our little artificial city on the tundra made. I glanced at Henry and then back at the administrator. "This is a day run?"

He nodded. "C-119 Boxcar and a Cat—worst-case scenario, a single overnight."

"On the big ice, on the day before the winter solstice, with three hours and forty-two minutes of daylight."

"Worst-case scenario."

"These must be important worms." I smiled.

Sanderson shrugged.

"Who's the pilot?"

"Bergstrom."

"The spotter?"

It was his turn to smile. "Blackjack," he said, as he left.

I glanced at Henry again, thinking this might be just the thing to keep him entertained. "What time?"

He called over his shoulder, his boots ringing in the hallway. "Wheels up at oh-five hundred."

"You wanted to see the Arctic." I pulled out two mugs from the top drawer of my desk and sat them between us, then retrieved a pint of Canadian whisky, extending the neck of the open bottle toward Henry, who placed a hand over his mug.

"You are slurring your words."

I stared at him for a moment and then poured one for myself, raising it in a toast. "I prefer to think of it as speaking in cursive."

2

Thunder Polar Pig was what they called her, and with good reason. She was loud, handled like a pig, and most of the guys said they'd dated her. She was a faded powder blue, and everyone assumed that she was a castoff from the United Nations, which she was.

The C-119 Flying Boxcar, a World War II–developed military transport, was famous for its clamshell openings in the back, where a Thiokol buggy sat chained to the floor. The Snowcat was somewhat vintage too, but a darker shade of blue, leading everyone to believe that it was a castoff of Sunoco, which it was.

For purposes of weight balance, the Cat was forward and the seven of us sat in the paratrooper seats in the back, facing one another in our immersion suits, which guaranteed to keep you alive in frigid water—at least for a couple hours longer than if you weren't wearing one.

I've been told that the clamshell doors on the C-119 seal, but they don't; they just kind of close enough to keep you from falling out. It was freezing cold back there, and in our immersion suits and parkas you couldn't tell who was who, but I already knew all of them but one—Henry; Roy Carlisle, the navigator; Mattingly, the radioman and flight engineer; the company man, Marco Vasquez; the spotter/shooter, Blackjack; and the USGS survey guy I knew only by his unique nickname. The pilot, Mike Bergstrom, and Jerry Boyle, the copilot, were up front.

I looked through the periscope of fox fur surrounding my tightened hood and found Henry seated in the tub beside me with the hood of his N-3B lowered. "Is it everything you hoped for in your wildest dreams?"

His eyes shifted to mine, but his head didn't move as he shouted back to be heard over the two Pratt & Whitney fourteen-cylinder engines that fought to carry us toward Santa Claus and the North Pole. "More."

Unbuttoning just enough to pull the metal flask from the mottled sealskin parka I wore over the immersion suit, which I had also inherited from my dead predecessor, I couldn't help but notice how much surplus surrounded us. It made me feel like I was back in the military. It made sense; the military or the big oil companies were the only ones who could afford to transport equipment like this to the ends of the earth.

My musings were broken as my attention was drawn to the individual sitting farthest from us, his hands folded around a .416-bore Rigby, the high-powered rifle with a massive scope that he cradled between his legs.

Blackjack was all I knew him by, and I wasn't sure if it was a nickname, a proper name, a first name or last name—or if it was an alias. He was a legend among the tight-knit group of professionals who made their living on the North Slope. In a world of renowned spotters, Blackjack was the best at what he did, and what he did was keep polar bears from devouring you while you did your work.

When we'd gotten on the plane in Nuiqsut, he had already been in here with the geologists from the U.S. Geological Survey. I had waved to the small man but he didn't move, and it was only later that I'd concluded he was sleeping.

He wasn't sleeping now and I still couldn't see his face, but I could tell by the way his head was cocked that he was watching me through his large yellow-tinted goggles. I unscrewed the top from the metal flask with an art deco design on the side and lifted it in a salute, but he simply turned his head toward the side window at the revolving propellers, which threw off ice in chunks that echoed against the fuselage.

Shrugging, I took a sip and then became aware of a gloved hand reaching across the cargo space. I lowered the flask and reached out to hand it to the skinny young USGS team leader called Wormy by his coworkers. I yelled to be heard over the clamor of the engines. "What they call you, is it a nickname or a condition?!"

Staring at myself in the reflection of his snow goggles, I watched as his lips parted in his struggling beard, revealing crooked but bright white teeth. "A nickname, because I work with worms!" I handed him the flask, which he took and upended before handing it back to me, sputtering in a New England accent. "That's terrible, what is it?"

I lowered my balaclava and shouted back. "A mixture of all the bottles that were left in my predecessor's desk." I screwed the top back on and tucked it away. "I call it Polar Piss."

He nodded. "Truth in advertising!"

"Yep, but if you do have worms that ought to kill 'em."

He shifted in his fiberglass seat and then unbuckled before standing unsteadily and traversing the catwalk over to our side and sitting beside me where we didn't have to yell. "So, you're the security guy?"

"I am." I extended a gloved hand, and we shook. "Walt Longmire."

"What are you supposed to be protecting us from, Walt Longmire?"

"Yourselves, mostly."

"Not polar bears?"

I threw a thumb toward the legendary shooter, now asleep again in the corner. "That's Blackjack's job."

Wormy nodded toward the Cheyenne Nation seated beside me, who watched us impassively. "I thought he was Blackjack."

"No, he's a buddy of mine from the Lower Forty-Eight vacationing up here."

The kid shook his head as if to clear it. "Who do you work for?"

I tipped my cowboy hat back and pulled away the sealskin parka, revealing the embroidered emblem. "Northstar."

"Oh, you're one of them."

"Meaning?"

"You work for the oil company."

"You don't?"

"No. Both the USGS and the National Science Foundation."

I gestured around the interior of the C-119. "Who's paying for the gas, the equipment, and us?"

He nodded and smiled again. "It behooves Northstar to stay on good terms with the NSF."

"How come?"

He stared at me. "You're new up here, huh?"

"Two months."

"Where, before that?"

"A little known country in Southeast Asia called Vietnam."

"Oh."

It was a loaded *oh*, but I was getting used to those and let it pass. "So why does Northstar care about the NSF?"

"We're good buddies with the EPA, Department of the Interior, Department of Energy, and people of the United States of America."

"Yep, I've been working for them for the last couple of years too."

He let that one pass. "Ever heard of the Arctic Refuge Proposition?"

"No."

"Neither have most people, but you're flying over it right now." He leaned in closer. "Stretching from the Beaufort Sea to the north, the Brooks Range to the south, and Prudhoe Bay to the west."

"What's to the east?"

"The Yukon Territory, Canada. You've heard of it?"

"Read about it in Jack London's books."

He nodded. "Your company wants some of the leases on this land, but we're working to have about twenty million acres deemed as a national refuge that won't allow any drilling at all."

"Okay."

He stared at me. "You don't care?"

"Not really, there seems to be plenty of Alaska to go around."

"There won't be."

"Meaning?"

"Energy dependence. We're consuming about twelve million barrels of oil a day, and it'll be a lot more by the end of the decade."

I shrugged. "So, we just import the stuff."

"For a while, yeah, but those areas in the Middle East are due for some political changes, and I don't think those people are going to want to give up their one bargaining chip for cheap. In the end, we're going to have to up production big-time, which means using every available resource, including what we're flying over right now."

"So Northstar is playing nice in hopes of getting onto your proposed refuge, which you're not going to let them do?"

"You got it."

"Good luck."

"What's that supposed to mean?"

"It means that money is power, and when you're up against big money like international oil companies, you're probably going to lose."

"Yeah, but we've got the government on our side."

"You think there's a difference?" I shook my head and smiled at the floor, watching my breath steam out and disappear. "Listen, kid, I just spent the last couple of years in Southeast Asia fighting a war and I'm not sure I understand why. I watched a lot of really great guys give up their lives and I'm not sure they understood either. All I do know is that money is power and power is money and if you yank back the sheets at midnight you're going to find them in bed together."

"That's a shitty attitude."

I leaned back in my seat, pulling the flask out again and raising it for another sip. "At least one tour in the making, but I think my personal philosophy has finally hit rock bottom."

"So, what do you believe in?"

"Human nature: if you set your sights low enough, it'll never let you down." I sipped again as Wormy stood, wavering with the turbulence as he made his way back over to his side and buckled himself into his seat, then pulled out a folder from a plastic container on the floor next to him. "What, we're not friends anymore?"

He began reading and ignored me as I noticed that Henry was giving me the hard eye. "What?"

He ignored me too, so I took another sip. "Fine, I'll drink alone."

As landings go, it was rough, but a landing nonetheless.

With the help of the copilot, Jerry Boyle, and the navigator, Roy Carlisle, we got to work constructing the spotter tower— a twenty-foot-tall lightweight metal device with something of a crow's nest at the top with a rotating seat and a shooting rail.

I noticed that Blackjack did not help but rather stood about fifty yards away, gazing northward at the frozen ice on which we now stood. "How come he doesn't help?"

"Heavy is the head that wears the crown." The Cheyenne Nation handed me another section, which I fumbled putting together with my thick gloves. "Because he is working. What if a polar bear decides to eat one of us while we are distracted? That is what bears do, in my experience."

"Ambush hunters?"

"Especially them." We constructed another section and then stood it up as Wormy and Marco attempted to unload the Thiokol, its treads flipping square bricks of ice and frozen snow in the air as they pulled it out and away from the Thunder Polar Pig. "Have you ever noticed that polar bears' heads are sleek and aerodynamic, unlike grizzlies'?"

Shrugging, I replied. "I can't say that I have."

"It is so they can go in the ice holes after six-hundred-pound seals and drag them back out—sometimes they wait for days." He gazed out at Blackjack, surveying the north. "These areas near the open sea are particularly dangerous because some of the bears have been stranded on ice flows with no food, and as soon as the flows bump into the mainland or larger pieces of ice, the bears start off, perhaps having not eaten for months."

"So, they're starving."

"Yes, and they do not care what they find—they will eat it."

"Including us?"

He grunted. "Especially us, since we do not have the finely honed escape skills of the seals."

I bolted together another section and we finished the tower as the NSF guy climbed up and began assembling the shooting seat and rail. "Where did you learn all this invaluable knowledge so quickly?"

The Bear raised a finger toward the figure standing in the distance with his back to us.

"Blackjack?"

He nodded. "A Yupik speaker."

"And you are too?"

"Enough that we can understand each other."

With the work done, we ambled back toward the aircraft and watched as the pilot, Mike Bergstrom, checked the gauges on the Arctic Cat and gunned the motor, helping it in its attempts to warm up. The heavyset Texan in the Northstar ball cap studied the dash and then looked up at a thermometer mounted on the outside of the windshield. "A balmy twenty-seven below; we'll be peeling down to our swimsuits before too long."

"What's the Cat for, Tex?"

"We're going to try to do two sites per stop. There's weather coming in tonight and I figured you guys would prefer to sleep at home rather than a tin can inside a tin can out here on the ice."

"You got that right." I turned to Wormy. "How far is the other site?"

"About ten miles."

"So, about an hour away."

"Yeah."

"How long will it take you to dig up your worms and put 'em in a coffee can?"

"Can't, above freezing they melt."

I grunted. "You know, the more you tell me about these worms the less interested I am."

Bergstrom shifted his dispassionate blue eyes toward me. "That's too bad since you're on the away team, here in Kitty One."

"And why is that?"

"Because you've got a rifle and know how to use it."

It was true that other than Blackjack, I was the only other official member of the party who was trained and armed, my M16 comfortably seated inside the C-119 in its winter cover. "You have any idea how many of those 5.56 × 45mm slugs you'd have to put in a polar bear to bring him to heel?"

"Let's hope you don't have to find out. Besides, you've got that ole .45, don't you?"

"If he gets close enough that I need to use it, I'll just shoot myself." I started in for my rifle and supply pack, calling over my shoulder, "Hey, Bergstrom, did you hear they're going to cut Alaska in half and name it the two largest states in America?"

The Texan nodded. "Good hunting."

Pulling up my gear, I turned to find Henry standing next to me. "Where do you think you're going?"

"With you."

"No, you might as well save yourself the torture and stay here. Those Cats have shitty suspensions and all we've got for lunch are MREs and some beef jerky—and you hate beef jerky."

"Not as much as I hate MREs"

I studied him back. "Are you babysitting me?"

"Possibly."

"For whom?" He didn't answer, and I knew better than to play the waiting game with the Cheyenne Nation—not that I had to anyway. "How is she?"

"Lonely."

I propped the covered M16 on my hip and tried to be a tough guy. "She'll get over it."

"Perhaps."

I nodded and stared past him, unable to meet his gaze. "Look at me, Henry, I'm a mess."

"Yes, you are, but a lot of us hope you will get better."

"Or worse." I thought about it. "I wouldn't wish me on my worst enemy." I finally sought out his dark eyes. "Seriously, how is Martha?"

"Wondering why she is in Wyoming while you are in Alaska."

"Look, I need some time."

"I thought we learned in Vietnam that time is the one thing we do not have."

I thought about it for a minute and then sidled by him. "Suit yourself." I pulled out my flask again and took a sip. "Just don't blame me if you get eaten by a polar." Following me as we clanked down the clamshell ramp, we watched as Blackjack climbed the ladder and took his position in the crow's nest, slowly circling. Tucking my flask away, I hoisted myself on the treads and yanked open one of the Thiokol's doors.

Henry grunted. "I will take my chances; I have a feeling you are more highly marinated, and they will choose to eat you."

Chugging along in the Cat with Wormy, Marco, and Henry, I soon found my head bumping against the glass as I drifted off to sleep, thinking about Martha. The last time we'd seen each other was in Honolulu, when I'd scored a two-week R & R.

It had been strange, or I had been strange, and we hadn't gotten along, spending a lot of our time avoiding each other and not saying anything. It was like we were strangers; we'd grown apart in the last few years and really weren't sure how to treat each other.

We'd parted ways as she'd gone back to Wyoming and I'd been posted to Johnston Atoll, punishment from the provost marshal for causing such a stir in my first homicide investigation back in Vietnam. Once there, I'd set pen to paper in an attempt to try to clear up our relationship when I'd received seven pages from her, echoing the same sentiments almost word for word.

I survived Johnston Atoll by the skin of many things, including my left hand, but when the time had come for me to return stateside, I'd taken a job with Northstar as a security consultant—and here I was. The money was good, but I wasn't sure the environs were beneficial to my mental health.

I had the feeling I was becoming unwound.

It was almost as if I couldn't go home, as if I wasn't sure who I was or that Wyoming was actually home anymore.

My head suddenly yanked forward as the Thiokol lurched to a stop, and we sat there, rocking back and forth on what little suspension the Arctic Cat had. "Are we there yet?"

Marco looked at me and the Bear as Wormy stared ahead, his long hair and scraggly beard unveiled in the warmth of the cab. "Yeah, pretty much."

Sitting forward, I reached into the back for my rifle. "So, hi-ho, hi-ho . . ." The two men in the front didn't move. "Is there a problem?"

Wormy nodded toward the windshield. "Yeah—him."

Leaning between the two seats, I stared out into the forever ripples of ice and snow, serrations of blue and white like giant corduroy. As my eyes began to focus, I finally saw something out there—a very large vertical figure in a horizontal landscape.

Standing over twelve feet tall if he were an inch, his massive arms hung easy, the claws in the giant paws highly noticeable from a hundred yards away, the sloped shoulders leading to the streamlined head and the tiny black spot that was his nose. The one eye was equally dark and stayed on us as the nose twitched and the head turned slightly, probably the first time he'd ever smelled exhaust fumes or metal.

Or men.

3

MOBILE OUTPOST 113, NUIQSUT, NORTH SLOPE, ALASKA

DECEMBER 22, 1970

His physical presence was intimidating enough, but it was the absolute nonchalance of the monster's movements that conveyed that he wasn't impressed with us, our vehicle, our weapons, or anything about us—he was the dominant, primordial king, and we were in his domain.

Nobody said anything, so I chimed in. "Why don't we just go somewhere else?"

Wormy shook his head. "Years of research went into picking this exact spot for the sampling; we can't just find another spot."

"You're telling me that the stretch of frozen ice a quarter of a mile to our left is any different from the stretch of frozen ice a quarter of a mile to our right or the stretch of frozen ice that we're sitting on right now?"

"Years of study . . ."

I slumped back in my seat, looking at Henry, who hadn't taken his eyes off the polar. "Horseshit."

The driver, Marco, a Northstar man who was older and a little rougher with a Fu Manchu mustache, gestured toward the bear. "Maybe we can wait him out?"

The Cheyenne Nation, our resident expert, lip pointed. "I do not think so, besides, it seems as if he has grown curious."

All heads turned in unison as the white giant slowly lowered himself down on all fours and began lumbering toward us, his great swinging head leading the way.

"Does this thing have a reverse?"

Marco slipped out a cigarette from a pack and lit one. "Two of 'em."

I turned to Henry. "How fast can polar bears run?"

"Twenty-five miles an hour."

I shifted my eyes to the driver. "And how fast will this thing go?"

"Twenty-four miles an hour, but we can do it longer . . . I think. At least until we run out of gas."

I rapped a few knuckles on the Plexiglas windows. "Well, I don't know about you guys, but I'm thinking we're Spam in a can in this thing, and I bet he's got lots of openers on the ends of those iddy-biddy widdle paws of his."

Wormy spoke to the group as the apex hyperpredator and the largest carnivore on the planet approached. "Any ideas?"

I studied the monster. "There's something wrong with that bear."

Henry leaned forward. "What do you mean?"

"He's not walking exactly straight, and one side looks . . . I don't know, wrong."

"He is malformed, and part of his fur is missing near the shoulder and neck."

When no one else spoke, I threw out a suggestion. "Circle this thing around about a quarter mile and see how interested he is. My bet is that he'll either get tired or bored or both and then we come back here and pull the samples on God's little acre and get the hell out of here before he gets back."

"And what if he continues to follow us?"

"We throw Marco here out on the ice and see if the bear likes Italian."

Marco shrugged. "I'm South American, and besides, I drive the Cat."

Wormy returned his focus back to the bear, now only fifty yards away. "I'm in charge."

I rolled my fingertips on the plastic stock of the M16 in my arms. "I've got the gun."

We all turned toward Henry Standing Bear, who shook his head. "It is always the Indian, is it not . . ."

The polar bear stayed within sight for about a couple of hundred yards as we'd rumbled along at an excruciating ten miles an hour, and I was pretty sure I didn't have any fillings left in my teeth as I spoke. "I don't see him."

"Neither do I." Marco swiveled his head, even going so far as to pivot the Thiokol and look back from whence we'd come. "And I'm not so sure that's cool, man."

I turned to Henry. "What do you think?"

He pointed slightly to the right where a higher level of ice had caught the snow, building up a ridge that tapered out about a half mile. "If I was hunting us, that is where I would be."

"You want me to drive over there?"

Henry reached to his side, pulling the handle of his door. "I do not think we would be able to sneak up on him in this."

Wormy looked at us incredulously. "You're not going out on the ice with that thing."

In answer, the Bear opened the door, ducked his head, and stepped out onto the treads, scanning the horizon as I skimmed across the seat, zipping up and shouldering my covered weapon, starting out after him. "Um . . . don't leave without us."

Wormy stretched back and handed me a Motorola. "At least take one of these."

Attaching the walkie-talkie to my parka, I pulled my goggles down over my eyes, then breathed in the subzero air, which I immediately coughed back out in the Cheyenne Nation's direction. "See him?"

"No, but if you are going to cough the whole time, he will probably find us rather quickly." He stepped off the treads and into the thin snow. "How thick is the ice here?"

"About three feet, give or take." I patted the treads on the Cat. "Thick enough to hold this thing."

"And the bear."

"I'm not sure which one weighs more." I watched as the Cheyenne Nation started off around the Thiokol to the right of the ridge. "Think the treads'll run over the bear if he's chasing us?"

He said nothing and continued on.

Unwrapping the M16 from its winter cover, I let the air breathe into the weapon to acclimatize it, as it had a tendency to be finicky in such conditions. "Hey, if this is your idea of babysitting . . . I've got to tell you; you are one horrible babysitter."

He ignored me again and walked toward the ridge.

I struggled to keep up. "How fast can a human run?"

"Top speed?"

"Yours."

He pointed to his Arctic boots. "In these, maybe twenty miles per hour—if highly motivated."

"Hmm . . . Seeing as how I wasn't the fastest lineman back at USC, I'm thinking I could do eighteen—if highly motivated."

He mumbled over his shoulder, "I think you are flattering yourself."

Figuring we were in the nontalking portion of the stalk, I clammed up and followed him closely as we eased to the top of the snow shelf, the wind having formed a knife's edge that thrust us about a foot out from the elongated drift. Watching Henry hunker down, I followed suit and we automatically looked in opposite directions and then switched, making sure one of us hadn't missed something.

Nothing.

We watched as a slight breeze swirled a little snow from the solid sea, lifting it in the air and then making it disappear like a magic trick.

Lowering my voice, I leaned toward him. "Maybe he gave up."

"Do you see anything else around here to eat?"

"Can't say that I do." I pointed toward another hump to the east a couple hundred yards away. "Possibly there?"

"Possibly."

I charged the M16 and flipped it onto single fire, figuring that if I had only thirty rounds, I wanted to make sure every one of them went exactly where I wanted them to go. "Where else could he be?"

"Good question." Stepping down the ridge, the Cheyenne Nation kept swiveling his head in all directions. It was possible that we'd outlasted the brute, but it was also possible that he was out here hunting us as we hunted him.

As I wrapped the strap of the Colt around my arm and I lifted the rifle, I thought about the manual I found in the armament locker with it—a paperback of notices from the Royal Canadian Mounted Police. The issued memos warned about keeping the parts properly lubricated and that condensation from moving from one temperature to another could cause the weapon to freeze. At the bottom, in pencil, someone had written in a whimsical hand, *Pee on it. No, really, it works!*

I tried to think what it would be like to take out your member in negative-twenty-seven degrees with a thousand-pound-plus bear charging at you, only to then take the time to urinate on your rifle—but I figured it would do about as much good as attempting to fire the thing.

"There."

I focused immediately to where Henry was pointing and could see an indentation in the snow at the bulge about a quarter mile away. Something was definitely different from the surrounding area, as if something was there or had been. "You think he's waiting over there?"

"Only one way to find out."

"Go back and climb in the Snowcat, and drive over?"

He shook his head as he stood up and started walking.

I followed, still keeping my head on a swivel. "Only a suggestion."

After about fifty feet, he lowered himself to the hard surface and took off a glove, spreading his fingers and feeling the cold. "No prints; the ice does not allow for it." His face rose within the coyote fur of his parka to frame a pair of ivory snow goggles, and I could've sworn I'd been transported back a few hundred years.

"Where did you get the antique eyewear?"

"From the ivory exchange in Anchorage."

I followed his gaze, the two of us surveying the Arctic expanse. "Where can he be?"

Knowing Henry Standing Bear as well as I did, his question sent a shiver through me that had nothing to do with cold.

He stood and we continued on, Henry keeping his eyes forward and me casting mine to where we'd been, figuring that if I were an apex predator going after another couple of apex predators, that was the way I'd be coming.

There was a crackling and then Wormy's voice carried from the handheld.

Static. "Hey, are you guys still alive out there, or am I talking to the inside of a bear?"

Without unclipping the thing, I depressed the toggle. "So far, so good, Kitty One."

Static. "Hey, we just got relayed a message from Northstar Base that the front is moving in faster than they thought and that we're going to have to get out of here pretty quick."

"What about your samples?"

Static. "Marco says we're about a half mile from the site."

"Hey, do me a favor and ask him what Fu Manchu is doing for facial hair this season?"

Static. "Mister Longmire?"

I keyed the mic. "So?"

Static. "So, ten minutes to get there, twenty minutes to get the samples, and then ten minutes to get back here."

"You're going to leave us out here on the ice?"

Static. "It's too rough to bring the Thiokol up there on the ridge where you are, and we'd just be wasting time trying. When you get done just circle back around and we'll pick you up after we get the samples."

I depressed the toggle. "And us out on the ice with that bear and nowhere to fall back to?"

Static. "I don't see how we have a choice. By the time you guys get back here we could be at the site."

I laughed, depressing the toggle again. "Well, we've dealt with worse. Circle back and get the job done—but don't forget about us. Tell Marco that if we have to walk ten miles in an Arctic storm with a giant polar bear chasing us, I'm going to cram this M16 down his throat."

Static. "Roger that."

"See you in forty minutes."

Static. "Roger that too."

I pulled the flask from inside my parka and took a sip. "Looks like it's just us."

Henry studied me. "And the bear."

"Possibly."

"Please stop drinking."

"Okay." I took a swig.

Without another word, he started off toward the bulge and I tucked away the flask, following at full trudge. "A jug of wine, a loaf of bread, and thou beside me singing in the wilderness."

"Have you ever seen anything like this before?"

"No."

The shell of snow and ice was broken like an egg and the inside was collapsed. "A den, possibly."

"A bear den?"

He reached inside, pulling up a chunk of ice and examining the hair attached to it. "Yes, I would say." He reached in again and pulled something else out that hung limp in his hand, slightly larger than a small dog, the eyes closed and the discolored tongue hanging from the side of its mouth. "Suffocated from the collapsed snow." Reaching in again, the expression on his face changed as he struggled with something, his armpit against the rim as he stretched his full reach, hauling another tiny body out. Placing this one in his lap, he began roughing the skin on the tiny creature and breathing in its face.

"What are you doing?"

"This one is still warm."

Kneeling down, I kept an eye out in all directions. "Do you think the one we saw was the mother?"

He continued scrubbing the tiny body, finally removing his gloves and holding it close to his face where he continued to breathe on it. "No, that one was definitely a male, but I can not imagine him tearing this den open and doing this." Exercising the tiny limbs, he doubled his efforts and was finally rewarded with a squeak.

We both started as the tiny thing squeaked again, turning its head to one side and sneezing and then yawning and looking up at the two of us like a diminutive animated toy bear.

"Did you just bring a polar bear cub back to life?"

"I think I did." As he cradled the little beast, we watched as it stretched its extremities and then curled into a natal ball. "Let me have your rifle cover."

I pulled the case off my back and handed it to him, watching as he wrapped the cub in the insulated material and then stood. "We must find the mother."

"What, you're running a polar bear adoption center now?" I was about to continue the diatribe when behind him, toward the base of the hillock, I saw a discoloration in the ice and shifting snow. "What the hell . . . ?"

My eyes followed the discoloration for about two hundred feet, ending in a clump that I was pretty sure was a dead polar bear. I stepped down, sinking a few feet into the dry snow that had engulfed the collapsed den. I struggled through the drift toward the smear where the stains continued and followed along, amazed at the amount of frozen blood.

The bear was lying on its side with multiple wounds to the head and neck; the heavy arterial bleeding soaked the ice around us a good ten feet in diameter. Its skull was crushed, and portions of its stomach and hindquarters had been eaten.

I looked up to find Henry surveying the grizzly scene. "The mother?"

"Yes."

"Cannibalism, is that normal?"

"No. There have been occurrences where the male kills

larger cubs so that they might mate with the sow, but not inside the den—and this one killed and then ate her."

"What about the ice floe thing? I mean, if they're starving . . ."

"The bear we saw was not starving."

"No, I suppose not—so maybe another bear." I watched as he knelt and felt the side of the dead creature. "Warm?"

"Yes." Cradling the rifle cover with the bear cub in it, he shot his eyes toward the distance, ever vigil. "At this temperature, I would say she has been dead for two hours or so."

I swept the horizon with my own eyes but could still see nothing. "What are the chances that it could've been something else?"

He slowly stood with the precious cargo and then took a few steps in front of the dead she-bear, carefully placing an oversize, insulated boot on the ground.

Stepping around the carcass, I walked over to where he stood, his lace-up Sorel dwarfed by a print at least twice as long and three times as wide, the claw marks sticking out like a set of dinner knives—obviously the bear we'd seen.

"I would say none."

4

MOBILE OUTPOST 113, OFF-SITE, NUIQSUT, NORTH SLOPE, ALASKA

DECEMBER 22, 1970

"How long has it been?"

"You're the one with the watch."

I waited as Henry risked frostbite and pulled up the sleeve of his parka to read the Seiko on his wrist. "It has been fifty-seven minutes."

Retrieving the M16 from under my arm, I turned in a circle, examining the sky and especially the bruising clouds that crowded out the blue to the northwest. "That front is coming in."

"Something has happened."

I pressed the toggle of the walkie-talkie and spoke. "Kitty One, where are you?"

We listened to the silence.

I hit the thing again. "Wormy, it's getting cold out here . . ." After a moment, I blew a cloud of vapor from my nose that crystalized in the air in front of me. "So, we have two choices: Either we head toward the sample site ten miles in that direction." I leveled a hand southeast, where the tracks of the Thiokol led below. "Or we just start for the plane, ten miles southwest." I pointed in that direction.

Henry nodded and stood from a kneeling position, pulling his hood in a little tighter. "How much time would you say we have?"

I studied the clouds again. "Weather changes fast up here, so I'd say less than an hour before it hits, at best."

"If Wormy and Marco have left us, for whatever reason, they would need to load the Cat and prepare for takeoff, which would require at least an hour, yes?"

I shook my head. "Bergstrom wouldn't leave us; he'd anchor the plane and wait it out."

"What if the Cat broke down or got stuck or ran out of gas?"

"It's possible, but if we get to the site and they aren't there, then it's a twenty-mile hike just to get to some cover."

"But, conceivably, we could get back to the plane in two hours and get off the ice and back to the rig where they may already be if we start walking now?"

"Yep." I gestured toward the cub, wrapped up in his arms. "Are you taking her with you?"

"I must, she will die out here alone."

I stepped off, leading the way southwest. "Let's try and not make it a club, shall we."

Skirting the ridge, we could feel a slight breath of a breeze steadily growing, and I wished we were on the other side of the ridge, which might've provided a little cover. The walking was actually good in that it produced a personal heat that was helpful, if not long-lasting—it might keep us warm until the storm hit, but after that we would slowly cool and be worse off than before.

I called over my shoulder. "So, what are you going to name her?"

"Martha."

I stared at him, but he simply continued on past me.

We'd gone a couple of miles when the gusts picked up, throwing shards of ice that cut like tiny needles. We began pulling our snorkel hoods and limiting our visibility to a circular hole about the circumference of a can of beans. "If that monster bear attacks us, do you suppose he'd be considerate enough to do it from directly in front?"

"Doubtful."

We both began rotating our heads with a little more alacrity. "At least promise me that if we are attacked, you'll throw him the cub?"

He hugged the bundle a little closer. "I intend to protect her with my life."

"What about mine?"

"You have the gun."

I pulled the thing out and examined it, thinking about all the ways the Colt rifle could malfunction in the cold. "How 'bout I throw a few rounds out of it, just to make sure it's still operable?"

"It may draw the bear to us."

"If he's within earshot, I'm willing to take that chance— I'd rather meet him with a working rifle than one that's frozen up." Clicking off the safety, I raised the barrel and pulled the trigger a few times, watching the flames leap from the muzzle as lead flew out at 3,150 feet per second. "It still works."

"With an effective point range of six hundred yards . . ."

"I'm betting I can put all twenty-seven remaining rounds in his ass and then I'll get out the .45."

"If properly motivated?"

"Exactly."

It was then that we heard a sound, two of them, off and to the left as we looked at each other, the Cheyenne Nation's hood opening a little larger than mine. "Was that a gunshot?"

I turned toward where the sounds had come from. "I think so." With Henry following, we trudged up the ridge to our left and had almost made it to the top when another one rang out. "That was definitely a shot."

Making the top of the ridge, we could see the bright blue Cat about a half mile away down the incline, pointed southwest, stopped with the engine panels exposed.

A man was standing in front of the snowmobile with a pistol held at arm's length. "That's ours, right?"

"I do not know who else would be out here."

"Only one guy?"

"Perhaps the other is under the hood."

I started off. "Well, let's go get some answers and maybe a ride—unless they shot the Thiokol to put it out of its misery and ours."

As we approached, I could see it was the driver who was holding a .357 on us. "Hey, Marco, long time no see."

He lowered the revolver, and I noticed that despite the temperature, he was sweating profusely and looked as if he might actually be in shock. "Thank fucking God, do you have any idea how long I've been out here waiting for you guys?"

I glanced back at the tracks leading straight toward the site. "About an hour, I'd guess. Where's Wormy?"

He laughed once and then began screaming. "What do you mean, 'Where's Wormy'? That . . . that *thing* got him!"

Henry pulled up beside me, and I took the pistol from Marco. "All right, calm down . . ."

The man gestured wildly, yanking his head in all directions. "Calm down? Calm down?! That fucking thing ate him, man! It ate him!"

"Settle down and tell me what happened."

"It ate him, man!"

I slapped him across the face, hard.

Falling against the tracks of the Thiokol, he wiped his mouth with the back of a glove and stared at me. "Don't you ever do that to me again."

"Take a breath and tell me what happened."

His eyes darted to Henry and then back to me. "That thing, that fucking bear came out of nowhere and grabbed Wormy. I mean, we were working the hole saw and the next thing I know that thing clamped its jaws into his shoulder, lifted him up, and then shook him like a dishrag." He was openly crying now. "Then it throws him on the ground and stands on him before crushing his head between its jaws like a melon, man. I mean I was standing there no farther than from me to you, and Wormy is screaming and flailing and I heard his skull pop."

"What'd you do?"

"What do you mean, what did I do? I ran for my life, man! I ran and jumped in the Thiokol and got the hell out of there!"

I held up the .357. "You had this the whole time?"

"Hey, fuck you, man. That bear was the size of a Pontiac and seriously messed up."

"What do you mean 'messed up'?"

"It wasn't covered in fur, it had skin patches, and its face was messed up with an eye missing, not like any other bear I've ever seen." He paused for a minute and then wiped some of the sweat away from his face. "So, where the hell were you, security man?"

I gestured to the greater expanse. "Out here, waiting for you."

"Fuck you."

Moving in closer, I stooped to examine the engine of the Snowcat. "So, what's wrong with this thing?"

"I don't know, it died or something. I just drive the thing, you know?"

After pocketing the revolver, I held my hand near the engine and sniffed. "You run this thing full out after you got in?"

"You bet your ass I did."

I climbed up on the track and then opened the driver's-side door and noted the gear selector. "Well, you must've panicked and left the thing in low and you may have burned up the engine." Flipping the ignition to accessory, I watched as the temperature gauge rocketed to the very top, pegging the needle. "Yep, it's overheated." I spotted the two-way radio, the mic cord dangling from the small ledge of the headliner. I grabbed the mic and tried to get it to show some sign of life. "Did you call base?"

"About a hundred times! But the damn thing doesn't work either."

True to his word, nothing was lighting up on the dashboard. "Must be some kind of short or breaker that shuts down the electrical system."

Henry stood behind the Northstar man and lifted up the bundle, parting it a little to peer in and warm it with his breath and bouncing it. "We have a choice to make."

"That, we do."

Marco's eyes darted between Henry and the bundle. "What is that?"

The Cheyenne Nation propped up the cub. "Her name is Martha."

Marco gave me a look. "What the hell, man?"

Ignoring him, I studied the machine. "Well, this thing might cool down pretty quick with the dropping temperatures and the engine panels open, or it might not start at all. In which case we'll need to walk the next ten miles." I glanced at the northwest skyline and the encroachment that seemed to be speeding up. "And with that storm coming in we might make it, or we might not, and I have to admit that I don't relish the thought of spending the night out in the open during an Arctic storm. Besides, if it starts, we could go back and retrieve Wormy's body."

Marco turned to me. "The hell with that, I'm not going back there. Did you hear anything I just said?"

"Yep, I did."

"There's nothing left, man. That thing ate him."

Henry looked back toward the site. "Bears do not eat the entire carcass in one sitting; they will feed and then return to the meal later."

"Even more of a reason to get the hell out of here!" Marco shook his head and reached toward me. "Give me my gun, I'm walking out."

I climbed down and faced the driver. "No, we stick together either here or walking, but nobody's striking out on their own."

"Gimme my gun, man."

"Look . . ." In a quick motion I came around with the stock of the M16 and planted it on the side of his head, whereupon he dropped like a sack of freeze-dried potatoes. "He was getting tiresome." I knelt down to check the unconscious man with the snot bubbles emitting from one nostril and then turned to Henry. "Don't you think he was getting tiresome?"

"Yes."

"Do you want to help me get him in the Cat?"

"You hit him; you carry him."

"Thanks."

I placed the matte-black mouse gun in the driver's seat, then lifted Marco and carried him around to the back, pulled the lever of the cargo door, swinging it wide, and then rolled him in. After pushing in a wayward leg, I closed the door and circled back around. I reached into the engine and turned the radiator cap with my heavily gloved hand, gently allowing some of the superheated vapor to escape.

Henry peered at me from the other side through the openings in the engine. "How long do you want to wait?"

"About ten minutes, then we see if she'll go, or we start walking." I nodded toward the unconscious man in the Cat. "And carrying."

"At least we will have something to feed the bear." He

straightened, and I was pretty sure he was looking at the sky. "How long would you say?"

"Less than an hour."

"Worse comes to worse, we can bundle up in here and spend the night."

He came around the front. "Sounds comfortable."

"Better than out in a snowdrift. You saw how that can end."

His eyes were drawn back to the sample site beyond the horizon again. "Hmm . . ."

I studied him. "Something?"

"Do you still have his weapon?"

"I do."

"May I see it?"

I pulled the revolver from the pocket of my parka and handed it to him as he transferred the bear cub to me. I held the surprisingly warm, little mass of snoozing fur as the Cheyenne Nation took off a glove to manipulate the .357, releasing the wheel and looking at the rounds nestled there. "How many times did he shoot to get our attention?"

"Three times."

He held the open cylinder out where I could see the depression marks the firing pin had made in the primers. "Then why have four rounds been fired?

On the third try, the engine caught and I breathed a sigh of relief into the cab, turning the interior heat to high and then reaching up to the dials on the two-way. "I was hoping that it was wired to operate while the engine was running."

Henry sat in the passenger seat, having unwrapped the cub that still lay there asleep. "And?"

"It's working."

"Why did it not it work for him?"

"He just drove the thing in a panic in low for miles, I'm not so sure he was in any shape to operate anything. Besides, he had it on the wrong channel." Pulling the mic, I switched it to our regular frequency and called in. "Northstar Base, this is Kitty One, over?"

Static.

"Northstar Base, this is Kitty One, over?" Reexamining the channel, I heightened the gain and waited a moment, pretty sure that I'd heard a faint signal call. "Northstar Base, this is Kitty One, do you copy?" Sure that I'd heard something this time, I readjusted again and the distant voice of Mike Bergstrom came over the airwaves.

Static. "Kitty One, this is Northstar Base, where the hell are you?"

I depressed the button on the mic. "Hey, Tex, it's Walt. We've got a problem . . ."

Static. "Yes, you do. If you don't have your ass back here in the next ten minutes we're here for the night."

"Then we're here for the night. Wormy's dead."

Static. "Come again?"

"Wormy, the USGS guy, is dead. Marco says a polar got him."

Static. "You've got to be kidding."

"Wish I was."

Static. "Where are you?"

"As near as I can tell we're about ten miles away. The Cat crapped out on mighty Marco, but we found him and got it running again. If we make good time, which I'm not promising because I think we're one overheat away from being a lawn ornament, we'll be there in less than an hour."

Static. "Then we're spending the night."

"We are spending the night."

Static. "We'll get started tying down the Thunder Polar Pig and buttoning her up."

"Roger that."

Static. "Did you say a bear?"

"I did, a very large one with a bad attitude."

Static. "God help us."

I hung the mic back and shoved the Thiokol into gear. "Boy howdy."

5

"I can't see a thing, how about you?"

"Me neither, and it appears to be getting worse."

Leaning forward, I squinted through the flat windshield of the Snowcat and watched as the intermittent wipers continued in their feeble attempts at clearing the glass. "Do you suppose this thing has rubber in the wipers, or is that just the arms dragging across the glass?"

"I would imagine that they are frozen and useless."

There was some noise from the back, and I was pretty sure that Marco was coming around, but I was busy negotiating the Cat with its duel yoke. "You know what would be handy in this thing?"

"What is that?"

"A compass." Reaching up, I plucked the mic from the Motorola and keyed it. "Northstar Base, this is Kitty One. You copy?"

Static. "You sound like you're right next to us. Go ahead, Kitty One."

"Mike, I don't suppose you guys can see us?"

Static. "Um . . . No. Are you guys lost, Walt?"

"Never lost, just powerfully confused." I keyed the mic again. "We've been traveling south-southwest as near as I can tell for the last forty minutes, and it sure seems like we should've been there by now, Mike."

Static. "Our visibility here is down to about twenty feet."

"Well then, we must be close. You'll let us know if we run into you, will you?" I peered through the windshield again and thought I might have seen something to my right, but that could've also been because I was hoping to see something to my right or anywhere else for that matter. "I don't want to overshoot you guys because as near as I can figure, it's a long way to Barrow."

Static. "Roger that."

Pulling the one lever and pushing the other, I pivoted the Thiokol back to the right and then straightened it out. Henry was fussing with the cub. "Hey, I could use a little help here?"

He looked up for an instant and then pointed a finger. "The plane is right there."

I followed his finger to the large, squat shape emerging from the dark and sighed. "Thanks a lot."

Bergstrom had done a good job tying the 119 down, but

the wind struck at the wings of the thing, pulling at it with alarming strength.

Driving the Thiokol right up to it on the ramps, I jammed the nose of the tracked vehicle against the clamshells in hopes that it might provide a little weight stability for the grounded bird.

Climbing out, we slid the side door back and I threw Marco onto my shoulder and grabbed the M16 as Henry wrapped up the cub and carried it ahead of us toward the portal door on the left rear of the plane.

We trudged our way forward and Bergstrom opened the hatch all the way, struggling to hold it as the wind continued battering us. Henry climbed in first, then reached out with another crewman and took Marco off my shoulder as I clamored in after them, falling to the metal floor and lodging the door shut with my boots.

Mike put a shoulder into it and wedged the hatch closed before spinning and hitting the two-point lever-latch and sealing it shut. "What the hell happened out there?"

I gestured toward Marco, who lay on the floor beside me, muttering to himself. "He says a bear got Wormy and that he had to make a run for it in the Thiokol, which he almost burned up. We found him out on the ice."

"A bear?"

I pulled my hood down. "Yep, I guess a bad one. We saw one while we were out, but then we saw the prints, much bigger than I've ever seen, out where a den had been broken into. The mother was killed along with one of the cubs . . ." I gestured toward Henry, who sat in one of the jump seats, uncovering the tiny polar. "We saved this one."

Mike shook his head. "Good grief."

I listened to the wind pounding the exterior of the fuselage as the Polar Pig jumped up and slammed back down on the ice. "What's our situation?"

"The front has arrived, in case you hadn't noticed, and we're grounded for a good twelve hours—that is, unless these katabatic winds from the shore join in with the vortex and pick this thing up and throw it out into the ocean."

"Which is covered in ice."

"Most of it, between here and eastern Russia, but the plates are shifting because of the wind."

Pushing myself back, I leaned against one of the supply crates and looked around. "So, in any case, we wait it out."

"Appears to be the situation." Mike sat in the jump seat next to Henry and stuck a finger out to the mewling cub. "We've got supplies enough for a good week in this thing, and I was able to get a signal through to an inland operation base."

"But nobody's going to be in the air for another twelve hours?"

"Including us." He shrugged. "If we get too much snow, we'll have to put the blade on the Cat and scrape off a runway to get out of here after we abandon it."

The ship was lifted again and then slammed back down as if being played with by an overly enthusiastic child. "Got 'er tied down good?"

"About a dozen eleven-inch ice screws, which should do the trick."

Mattingly, a young guy with long red hair I'd seen on the flight, came over and stood beside Bergstrom. "Sorry, but you said to tell you if it was still there."

Mike nodded. "You're sure it's not terrain masking?"

The radioman laughed. "From what, the twenty-foot drifts we've got out there?"

"You mark it?"

"I did, it's about a mile away, due northwest."

"Anything on the radio?"

"Nothing."

"You tried all the frequencies?"

"Working on it."

"Thanks, Matty. Good to know if things get bad."

After the young man left, I asked. "What's that all about?"

Mike sighed. "Matty picked something up on the terrain following radar—TFR—a blip that might be a ship to the northwest of us. He's trying to raise them on the radio, but so far, nothing."

"Think it's real?"

He smiled. "I'd hate to have to depend on a shadow in the radar for our survival."

"Amen to that, brother." I nodded toward Marco, who had yet to move. "You wanna help me get Mario Andretti in a sling and covered up?" I heaved myself to a standing position and lifted the unconscious man by the shoulders as Mike took his legs, and we carried him over to a cargo net that had been strung up like a hammock. We placed him in there with a blanket and returned toward the front of the plane as Henry continued to hold the cub like a child before getting Bergstrom's attention. "Do you have any milk?"

The Texan smiled, adjusting his cap and shaking his head. "Condensed, in the commissary locker, but we don't have a bottle, or a nipple for that matter."

The Cheyenne Nation smiled back. "We will make do, under the circumstances."

The wind lifted the plane again, slamming it back onto the ice. "I sure hope those ice screws hold, otherwise we're going to have a short and violent flight." I peeked around the rifle cover at the closed eyes. "Twenty pounds?"

"About that. I would say her eyes have not been open very long." He nodded toward the spotter, who was once again sleeping in a seat across from us. "Blackjack says that the females do not truly hibernate, but after giving birth they den up for three months before becoming active again."

I slumped back in my seat. "That bear out there, why would it cannibalize the female and then attack Wormy no more than a few hours later?"

"Bears can be opportunistic, but this one does not seem to behave like a normal animal."

"When we first saw it, it looked . . . I don't know, deformed?"

"Possibly a birth defect, or it had met with some kind of accident."

"What are the chances that a bear could be born like that and still survive to adulthood?"

"Not very good, I would think."

"Me neither." I pulled out my flask and took the last swig. "Well, here's to adventure."

There was another great gust as the Thunder Polar Pig again leapt from the ground. It didn't slam down immediately but instead hovered for a second before hammering back to earth, consequently throwing me to the metal floor.

"This is going to be a long night." I lay there for a minute and then rolled over to face Henry. "Is it me, or are those gusts getting stronger?"

The small bear in his lap howled as Henry covered it again with the rifle wrap. "Definitely stronger."

Mike appeared with the can of milk, handing it to the Cheyenne Nation, and we watched as he expertly opened it with his stag-handled bowie knife. "I think we're going to have to check those ice screws. I'm afraid they might be loosening."

"What's this *we* shit?"

He sat in the seat beside me, head down. "Well, if you're not so drunk you can't stand, I could use a little security backup."

I threw a thumb toward the amazingly still-sleeping, small man in the corner. "Take Blackjack."

"He's sleeping. Besides the wind'll blow him away."

He had a point. I stood and placed the M16 on the seat

beside Henry and pulled my .45 out and checked it. "Anybody else have a handgun? I'm not bothering with this damn rifle because I know it'll freeze up."

"There are two short-barrel 29s in the cockpit."

".44s?"

"Yeah."

"Now you're talking. Bring 'em back and I'll take one instead of my .45."

"What about the other one?"

I gestured toward the Cheyenne Nation. "Give it to him, that way if we don't come back, he'll have something to defend himself with."

He made a face but went back and got the guns along with a few headlamps, distributing them between us as he zipped and buttoned up. I got myself ready to face the elements as he grabbed a steel bar from a tool chest at the rear of the compartment.

"You're going to tighten those things down with that?"

"All we've got. I can't get the pneumatic wrench and generator out in this."

"Right." Moving toward the rear hatch, I saw Mattingly coming back, holding a piece of paper.

The young man handed it to Bergstrom, and he looked at it before handing it back to him. "So?"

"It's still there on the radar . . . It's a ship I'm telling you."

Mike cinched down his hood, adjusting his goggles and headlamp, then handed me mine. "How far?"

"Like I said—about a mile, I'd guess."

A gust came up, shuddering the plane again, but this time pushing down on it. "In this shit? It might as well be a hundred."

The young man sighed, taking the paper and moving toward the front as Mike turned to me. "He wants to go out and see if he can find this imaginary ship."

I opened the Smith & Wesson and checked the load, then closed it and held it to my chest where it might stay a little warmer. "In the dark, in a blizzard, with a man-eating bear out there?"

"He can be a little wifty sometimes." Bergstrom switched on his headlamp, which reminded me to turn mine on, and then put his hand on the lever to prepare to open the hatch. "Tomorrow we're going to have to go out there and locate Wormy's body."

"Or what's left of it, Tex."

"Tell me, did you develop this finely honed sense of humor of yours in Vietnam?" Without waiting for an answer, he turned the lever and wedged himself in the doorway as I lowered my own goggles and quickly followed.

Leaning against the fuselage, I slammed the hatch shut and continued after Mike as he made his way along underneath the wing.

He was only twenty feet away and I could barely see him as he felt for one of the guidewires and knelt beside it with the tool he had brought.

I moved next to him as he struggled to turn the thing, but it wouldn't budge. I started to reach down to give it a try when I thought I saw something move just beyond the visibility of my headlamp, but snow darted in and out of the light, and I couldn't see anything. Redirecting my attention back to Mike, I watched as he continued to struggle with the ice screw. Finally, I knelt down and shouted in his ear, or where his ear would've been inside the insulated hood. "Forget it, if they're in that tight, you're never going to get them any tighter! Let's go check some of the others!"

He nodded and stood with me as we turned, both figuring we'd check the other wing first. Crossing toward the front of the plane, we dipped underneath the nose and started out just as something came whistling through the air, striking Mike in the side of the head.

He dropped to the snow as I raised the Smith & Wesson, aiming it into the beam, but there was nothing there. I waited a second and then started to kneel down just as something struck me in the head, bursting my headlamp.

Reaching out, I grabbed at whatever it was, aiming the big revolver in all directions. Pulling the thing to my face, I could see it was one of the foot-long ice screws with the cable guideline still attached, and there was blood on it.

Tucking it under my boot so that it wouldn't get immediately free, I pulled the Texan to one side. His headlamp was broken too, and his face was completely covered by his hood but I knew he was hurt. I grabbed his arm and swung him around, dragging him toward the main body of the plane when we were both suddenly stopped.

Figuring I must've hung him up on the landing gear, I

pulled again but nothing happened. Yanking at him, he still didn't move, but suddenly he lurched the other way, dragging me with him.

Falling forward, I peered into the darkness but couldn't see anything as I held on to him, raising the pistol and firing.

Nothing. Only the stinging of the snow and incessant howling of the wind.

I knelt down and kept the .44 pointed in the same direction, then grabbed Bergstrom by the hood and dragged him with me as I scrambled backward, keeping the revolver leveled at whatever was out there.

Finally getting to the hatch, I pulled the lever and found that it was locked.

I tried it again, but it still didn't budge.

Glancing behind me, I could've sworn I could see something moving in the darkness. I rested Mike against my legs as I began banging on the side of the plane. "Open the door!"

There was no response as I continued to beat on the aluminum, so I started hammering the hatch with the butt of the revolver. "Open the damn door!"

There was a quick movement, and I felt the weight of Bergstrom's body removed from my legs. Figuring he must've fallen over, I turned to grab him.

And he was gone.

The hatch banged open behind me, and in the available light I could see nothing but a slight indentation in the snow and a small trail of blood where it looked like Bergstrom's body had been dragged away.

I took a step forward but then felt someone grab me by the shoulders and wrench me up into the plane, the two of us falling backward as another individual scrambled into the opening to hold the hatch open. Jerry, the tall, bald co-pilot, screamed over the wind. "Where's Mike?"

"He's . . . he's gone, he's gone. He was there with me one moment and the next, he just disappeared!"

Henry sat me up from where he'd pulled me in. "What happened?"

I lunged toward the door, but Henry held me fast.

Jerry was now hanging out of the hatch, holding on to the door and trying to see through the wind and snow. "Where is he?!" He started pulling himself back in when the wind slammed the door partially shut behind him.

"One of the ice screws came loose and hit Mike, knocking him unconscious. I was dragging him in when something snagged him. I shot at whatever it was, but it didn't make a sound—I mean nothing. I pulled him to the door and when I turned back from banging on it, he was gone." I scanned the faces at the assembled men, breathless. "Who the hell locked the door?"

The navigator, Roy, was now sitting in the seat next to the hatch, holding the baby polar bear. "Nobody, nobody locked it."

Marco, having now recovered, stood to the side. "It's that monster, I'm telling you!"

Jerry continued to struggle with the hatch lever, squinting through the blistering snow and wind as Roy handed the bear cub off to Henry and grabbed hold of him, pulling him inside and enabling the door to shut. Roy quickly secured the hatch as the copilot turned on him.

"Mike's out there, we have to go get him!"

Marco stepped in closer, putting his face to the porthole. "He's gone, man. If that thing was out there, then he's gone."

Jerry stabbed him with a forefinger. "You shut the fuck up, passenger!"

Marco barked a laugh, one without much humor. "You didn't see that thing; you have no idea . . ." He turned to me. "You shot it?"

"I think I did. I mean if it had him it was at point-blank range, and I don't see how I could've missed."

Roy moved closer to the door. "But you didn't see it?"

"No, I didn't see it, but I felt it when it first got ahold of Mike and I'm telling you that when I turned around, it was gone in an instant." I lurched forward, catching Henry off guard, and struggled to a standing position in order to grab the handle on the door. "I'm going back out there."

Roy shoved himself between me and the hatch. "No, you're not."

"Look, Mike may be lying out there, so I'm going after him."

"No. We've already lost one and possibly two men—we're not going to lose a third."

I tried to turn the lever, but the smaller man was lodged in front of me, adjusting his thick glasses. "What if he's still alive?"

"He's not alive, man. Not if that thing got him, and what

else could be out there?" Marco moved against the far wall as the Cheyenne Nation cooed at the bear cub.

"They are right. If it was the bear, then he is dead."

"This doesn't make any sense, Henry, bears don't act this way—they kill for food and this one's already killed a full-grown sow as well as a person, according to Marco here. Why would it continue killing?"

"Because it is not a bear." We all turned to the unfamiliar voice, finding Blackjack standing in the center aisle, pointing the .416 Rigby toward us. Carefully reaching up, the surprisingly delicate hand drew back the fur-lined hood to reveal that he, Blackjack, was a woman.

6

MOBILE OUTPOST 113, OFF-SITE, NUIQSUT, NORTH SLOPE, ALASKA

DECEMBER 22, 1970

There was another gust as something struck the side of the plane, something metal, followed by a grinding noise as it struck again, and I figured it was the ice screws and attached guidelines scraping along the fuselage.

Marco looked back at the group and then again to the spotter, still holding the rifle on us. "Wait, you're a chick?"

She shook her head, stepping forward and lowering the barrel of the high-powered Rigby. "Did you hear anything I said?"

He stared at her. "Yeah, but you're a chick?"

She glanced at Henry, who shrugged at me. He was still holding the cub. "The ice screws are pulling loose on the port side?"

I waved him away with a hand. "I'm going out there to find Mike."

She moved toward me. "If it is what I believe it is, you will die."

I shook my head. "I don't particularly care if it's the Grand Imperial Pooh-Bah of all polar bears, you don't leave a man behind."

"It may very well be."

The dragging noise struck the side of the fuselage again, the twisting braided cables against the aluminum side to our left screeching like metal fingernails on a chalkboard. The big C-119 leapt again but immediately slammed back onto the ice hard enough for my knees to buckle.

The Cheyenne Nation stepped between Blackjack and me, glancing at us and then at the copilot. "If this plane becomes loose, we will all die, yes?"

Jerry nodded his head emphatically. "It's likely."

He faced me. "Then that must be our first concern, agreed? Then we can try to find Mike, but it is dark and a raging blizzard outside, so I must tell you that I do not hold out much hope."

"You'll come with me?"

He smiled, walking over to Blackjack and handing her the cub as it struggled inside the rifle cover. She examined it with a sense of apprehension. Joining me at the hatch, the Cheyenne Nation pulled the matching .44 from inside his parka and then re-zipped. "But of course."

We'd just started to open the hatchway when the tone of

the wind changed . . . at least I thought it was the wind. It was different this time: a roar from the far distance and steady, like a wave—one that was growing.

I thought I might be the only one hearing it when I turned to Henry, whose eyes had widened. "Grab ahold of something!" He scrambled toward Blackjack and took the cub from her. "Get in the seats and buckle up!"

Most got to the seats as the first part of the gust hit, but Jerry was attempting to get to the cockpit when the C-119 lifted from the ground again, the wind this time pivoting to the starboard side and lifting the plane's tail. He flew through the air, slamming into the chromate-green bulkhead and then landing unceremoniously at the foot of the small steps that led to the cockpit of the plane.

The weight of the Thiokol Cat held the ramps at the rear, but only for a moment as the gust increased and the starboard side began lifting even higher.

I hadn't gotten into a seat but was holding on to one of the bracing bars beside the side hatch, just hoping I could hang on. Marco, thinking the worst was over, began unbuckling his belt as I yelled at him. "Stay seated!"

The gust grew, sounding more and more like a freight train—and slamming the transport like one too. There was a torquing sound from the rear, and I was pretty sure that before long the weight of the Cat was either going to tear the loading ramps off the plane or flip along with us.

We got our answer as the cargo plane lifted farther from the ground and started to turn over. The sound was tremendous as metal screeched and the thing flung itself up and cart-wheeled, slamming against the ice upside down as all the items in the cargo racks broke loose and flew around the inside like a maelstrom.

My grip pried open and I came free, bouncing to the roof before sliding toward the clamshell doors that now hung slightly ajar when all the flotsam and jetsam in the plane began moving again, skimming to the port side before lurching to a stop with a sudden yank.

Amid the chaos and noise inside, I was pretty sure some of the ice screws must've held, and because the high-center-of-gravity wings of the C-119 were now lying flat on the ice with no way to catch the wind, it was possible the ride was over—for now.

Sitting up, I pushed some of the cargo aside as a wooden crate fell from the floor above and crashed onto the ceiling where I now sat, missing my legs by only a few feet as the net tangled around my boots. "Stay where you are, it might not be over!"

Everybody quieted down, most still hanging from the harnesses, though part of Blackjack's had broken loose. Henry still hung there with the cub in his arms, who was now squealing and kicking.

The gusts stayed steady, and I could feel a jostling as the guidelines tethered out to their full length and bumped as the ice screws attempted to hold. Though I didn't figure we'd lift again, it was possible that we'd continue sliding if the few remaining screws broke loose.

I'd just stood up when they snapped free like gunshots. The plane shuddered a bit and then began moving again, slowly at first but gaining momentum as we vibrated along.

Roy called out. "We're moving!"

I would've thought that the weight and mass of the snow carpet would've slowed us, but the craft kept grinding along for what seemed like multiple lifetimes.

"Are we still moving?" Marco was looking around, panicked.

"Yep and stay where you are! The safest place in this thing is in those jump seats!"

The gust began to subside a bit until suddenly the cargo plane lodged against something, coming to a soft stop. The door behind me lurched open and fell partially away, dropping onto the twisted ramp, where the Cat was nowhere to be found.

The wind howled inside as if attempting to get hold of us as I shoved the crate in that direction, wadding the netting and stuffing it in the space to try to block out the elements, but it wasn't much use.

Henry had also freed himself and was walking toward me with the cub, going so far as to hand her to me. "Here, bear-sit."

I took her and then walked past him as he helped the others, kneeling by Jerry long enough to turn him over and ascertain that he was still breathing. I slapped at his face until he finally came around, knocking my hand away. "What happened?"

"We took that short, violent flight you were talking about."

I handed him the cub. "Here, hang on to her while I get the rest of the bats off the ceiling."

I stood and turned, finding that Henry had already done most of the work.

After helping Blackjack out of the broken harness where she hung like an unstrung marionette, I swiveled around toward our motley crew. "Everybody okay, considering?"

Marco, of course, was the first to speak. "What the hell happened?"

"She flipped, and as near as I can tell, the wind must've pushed this thing about a mile to the east after the guide-lines broke."

Matty pulled his hair from his face and interrupted. "Northeast."

I glanced at the others and then back at him. "Where the hell have you been?"

"You said for everybody to belt up, so I did at my station in the cockpit so I could try to get a signal out or read the instruments."

"And?"

"Nothing. The radio, the TFR, it's all dead—which shouldn't come as too much of a surprise in that every bit of electronic equipment and aerials on the top of this thing probably got scraped off in the ride northeast."

"Which means?"

"We're at least a mile out on the ice pack." He swallowed. "Where we were working before the ice was about four feet thick, but out here, who knows?"

"But strong enough to hold the plane, right?"

"I don't know. With the wind and the ocean moving it could be thin out here, along with the shelf drift this near the shore that's likely breaking it up."

"So, you're saying this thing could sink?"

He nodded. "It's possible, yes."

"Holy hell!" Marco stepped back in terror. "You have got to be kidding me?"

Embarrassment washed over the flight engineer's face. "Wormy wanted to be as close to the shoreline as possible, and we all thought that a mile from the edge would be sufficient."

"But it's not?"

He turned toward me. "It was until the wind pushed us out here on the edge."

Marco's voice became pleading. "What about the Cat, can't we use it?"

"The Cat is gone." I addressed the others. "Well, we won't last an hour out on the ice with nothing to break this wind, so as near as I can tell we just have to stick it out in here."

"Walt?"

Henry was at the back of the plane near the clamshells with Roy, both of them studying the floor. I held up a finger then moved in that direction as the others argued among themselves.

When I got there, the Bear pointed to the subceiling underneath the grating where water freely lapped against the metal structure. "Well, horseshit—is there one more thing that could go wrong in this little misadventure?"

He smiled his paper-thin smile. "Possibly."

"How long?"

Navigator Carlisle was the first to answer. "Difficult to say, but with the weight of the plane and the hot spot we're providing that's weakening the ice . . ." There was a sudden jarring as the starboard side of the plane suddenly sank about a foot. "There's your answer."

Henry grabbed a rail and looked worriedly at the others. "I would say the heat signature of our right engine just made itself known."

"What the hell was that?" Marco moved in our direction. "And what are you guys over here whispering about?"

I spoke over him to the others. "I think we better consider what we're going to do about getting out of this leaking ship."

Matty was the first one to pass Marco and see the water, which seemed a little deeper. "Oh, shit . . ."

"The Cat! We should hop in the Cat and get the hell out of here and back on dry ground."

I turned to him. "Marco, the Cat is about a mile that way and that's if it's sitting upright and still operable, which I seriously doubt."

The others crowded nearby. "What are we going to do?"

"The shadow."

I shook my head at Matty, raising an eyebrow. "Lamont Cranston, the comic book character?"

"No, no . . . The shadow on the TFR, the ship I saw that

was to the northeast on the radar before we rolled? It's out here somewhere."

"You're kidding, right? There's no way we're going out in this stuff to wander around searching for a ship at sea."

He looked down at the increasing water at our feet. "What else can we do?"

"Stay here!" Marco pleaded with the others. "I'm not going out with that thing still out there, whatever it is, the hell with that."

I raised my hands in an attempt to get everybody under control, speaking to Blackjack who stood at the rear, now holding the cub but saying nothing. "Hey, what are the chances that bear followed us?"

She shrugged, her dark hair parting enough to reveal one dark eye. "Not very good, *if* it was a bear, it would've been frightened by the plane turning over and all the noise."

"What is this 'if' shit?"

Ignoring Marco, I glanced back down at the water, noting another increase as the plane shuddered once more. "That settles it: Henry and I will go out, get a read on the area, and see if we can find someplace we can use as shelter."

"Why you two?"

"You wanna go out there?" Buttoning up my parka, lowering my goggles, and cranking down my cowboy hat and tightening the stampede straps, I squared off with the mouth. "We're all going to be out there in about an hour, trying to survive." He had nothing more to say to that, so I spoke to the others. "Okay people, listen up. We've got about fifty minutes or less to gather our stuff and get out of here. Get suited up for the ice and bring along everything you think might be useful."

Marco jockeyed for my attention. "Yeah, but what if it doesn't sink?"

"Then we've gotten ready in case it does. Personally, I don't want to be forced out there when I'm not ready. How 'bout you?" There was no more talk, and I quickly packed a rucksack as the others began gathering their things along with survival equipment, the majority of which had fallen from the racks. "Hey, does anybody have an extra head-light?"

Roy pulled his from the pocket of his parka and handed it to me. I strapped it on my head and then cranked down my cowboy hat again and drew the .44 from the inside pocket of my parka. Cinching my hood down around my neck, I looked through the fur at Henry, who was doing the same. "Ready?"

He tugged on his gloves, then pulled his own revolver out, his breath clouding the air between us. "As I will ever be."

I turned toward the others. "Okay, dump all you can out of the clamshells after us. It's the largest opening, but if this thing starts to go—get the hell out of here." As I picked up my rucksack from the floor, I noticed the bottom was wet before slinging it onto my shoulder along with the M16. I briefly glanced back with longing at Blackjack and my rifle cover that was cradling a polar bear cub, then I pulled the cargo netting out of the way and pushed past the crate and into the opening of the clamshell doors.

The wind was still blistering as I stepped gingerly on the ice, hoping I wouldn't disappear into the dark depths. Satisfied it was relatively stable, I took another step out and could vaguely see the twin tail structure lying on the ground in the blowing snow and darkness.

I stepped onto the tail section and clicked on my headlight, noting the clawlike scratches in the aluminum. I knelt and pointed it out to Henry, spreading my fingers, attempting to match the spread of the claws but only covering slightly less than halfway. I yelled to be heard as he knelt beside me. "Look like bear to you?!"

"Possibly, but larger than I have ever seen!"

I nodded and redirected my headlamp past the wreckage. I could make out the ramp section about forty feet away, where it had gotten tangled in the guidewires and dragged along behind us.

"No sign of the Cat!"

He was standing beside me. "Did you think there would be?!"

"Would've been close quarters with seven of us in that thing." I took a few more steps out but then decided there was little use going the way we'd slid, figuring there was nothing but flat ice and wind in that direction. I started making my way around the tail section and feeling my way along the fuselage, quickly coming to the hatch at the side, where the Cheyenne Nation had pulled me in.

I could see more scratches. "What about these?" There was no answer, so I turned back where he had been. "Henry!"

Shining the headlight in all directions, I could see no sight of him. I felt my hand tightening around the .44, and I cocked it. "Henry!"

Nothing.

Easing back along the aluminum side of the cargo plane, I got to the edge of the clamshells when something came through the air, falling to the snow-encrusted ice.

Supplies.

The others were throwing things out onto the ice.

Breathing a sigh, I circled around looking for prints, but the ongoing wind filled them up as fast as you could make them; besides, I didn't like the idea of spending my time out there with my head down.

I got to the other side, careful to circle around the clamshells and piles of stuff that were accumulating and could now see Henry standing on some piled-up chunks of big ice.

Trudging along after him, I could see that the dip in the wing had come from the engine on that side, indeed breaking through and sinking. We were going to have to get a move on getting whatever we needed out of the plane—wherever we were going.

"Hey!"

He stood there on the small promontory and was staring off into the distance.

I sloughed through the final distance to get to where he was standing and tugged on his sleeve.

"Nothing?" He still didn't respond as I stepped beside him, shining my headlight out into the grayish-black distance that seemed to cover the impossible vista without revealing a single feature. "Jeez, it's like looking at a steel wall."

"Yes, it is." He reached out a gloved hand and pounded as the landscape gave out with an unearthly echo.

Stunned, I stepped back and allowed my headlamp to climb and climb, finally reaching the ghostly words stenciled across the broad steel transom.

SS

BAYCHIMO

LONDON

7

"Freighter?!"

Moving to the side, I shined the headlamp down the length of the thing, only reaching about twenty feet as I continued to yell. "A small tramp steamer, yes!" Henry looked at me and I shrugged in response, slapping him on the back. "Comparatively speaking!"

At the far end of the beam, something moved in the gloom. "Rope ladder!"

"Hanging from the side?" He joined me in looking up and onto the decks. "Do you see any lights on board?"

"No!" Shining the headlight, I could see built-up ice on the railings blown out from the wind like knife edges at least a foot long. "She's in rough shape, but any port in a storm!" I pulled on his sleeve. "Come on, let's get the others!"

He lingered there for a moment and then continued along the side.

"Where are you going?!" He ignored me and went toward the rope ladder. "Be careful on the broken ice, you can slip through in an instant!"

I returned to the level ice where I tromped over to the clamshells and lodged myself into the opening, sheltered enough to raise my goggles and yell inside at the group now clustered there. "You're not going to believe this, but the ship that Matty was ghosting on the TFR is right outside and probably the reason the ice is breaking up around the plane— also why we stopped sliding and didn't end up somewhere in the Arctic Sea."

Jerry, now with a bandage wrapped around his head, moved in closer. "Can they send some people down to help us?"

"We haven't seen any lights on board, but they could just be covered with ice."

Matty moved closer, unable to keep the smile from his face. "I knew there was something out there."

"Load up all the stuff, it's bound to be colder than a well digger's ass, but at least we can get out of the wind! Get your immersion suits zipped and sealed tight. The ice around the ship is all broken up and refrozen, but who knows if it's stable!"

Pulling back, I threw another sack over my shoulder and started toward the ship. Henry was nowhere to be seen, but

I figured he must've climbed the rope ladder and onto the above deck.

Shining the light in that direction, I crossed farther down the hull and could see a notch where a gangplank must've rested and a hump in the broken ice that made for a natural ramp. I figured I could just sling my stuff up on the deck and go back for more.

I'd just thrown up the first load when I saw something move into the opening, and the Cheyenne Nation reached down to take the supplies I'd tossed, including the rifle.

"Been exploring?"

He knelt, taking the rest from me as he yelled back. "There is no one on board!"

"No one?!"

"No one, and she appears to have been abandoned for some time!"

"Is the bridge intact?"

He nodded. "There are windows broken out in the fore-castle, but the captain's quarters and mess appear to be solid! There must be ice a foot thick all over her!"

"I'll get the others and bring them this way with the supplies! Is the rope ladder safe?"

"Yes, amazingly enough!"

Tramping back toward the plane, I ran into the first group with their arms loaded. "Go farther down the hull and there's an opening onto the deck! Henry is there and can help take the supplies, but be careful because the ice is un-even!" They made their way toward Henry as I went back to the plane, where I could see Roy and Blackjack with the polar cub.

I paused to give them the same directions and continued toward the clamshells where Marco stood in the plane, buttoning up his parka. "There's really a ship out there?"

"Yep, an old freighter—really old, like the early part of the century."

"But they'll help us?"

I gathered a few more items and some of the emergency rations that had spilled out from the main containers that the others had already taken. "It's abandoned."

"What do you mean 'abandoned'?"

I straightened, noticing he wasn't carrying anything. "As in, there's nobody on the damn thing."

"What good is that gonna do?"

"It'll keep us out of this wind, and it'll float better than this plane, I can guarantee you."

He looked down at the advancing water and then back over my shoulder to the southwest. "I may go after the Cat, I mean, at least it's got a radio that works . . ."

"You'll die in the process; that thing's at least a mile away, and we don't know in what direction or what condition it's in." I played my hole card to the max. "Besides, there's that bear, and he'd love to find some poor guy out there stumbling around all by himself."

That gave him pause.

"Anyway, I'm headed in, and I think I'm the last, so after this you're on your own."

I'd started to turn when he called out. "Wait!"

I gestured toward the supplies scattered on the floor. "Get something to put that stuff in and follow me."

He did as I said and tagged along as we made our way around the clamshells toward the hull of the ship. The snow had given us a brief respite, and I could see maybe another twenty yards more than before, but the vision wasn't uplifting.

As near as I could tell she must've been commissioned sometime after the turn of the century, steam-powered and not large enough to work the open waterways. She was a scavenger, probably used somewhere else until after her prime and then sent to ply the Arctic seas, dodging the ice floes every winter. Her profit margin likely depended on her working dangerous areas, providing supplies to the settlements from the North Slope to Siberia or possibly hauling goods—but what?

Some of the lead lines still hung from the rear stack and the two masts forward where a tower sat amidships, completely covered in at least three feet of solid ice. All the lifeboats but for one scow were missing, the larger boat hanging from the heavy lifting gear and swinging above a cargo hold, leading me to believe that there must've been some kind of disaster, or maybe someone else on board had been attempting an escape.

But why leave the one lifeboat hanging out here?

"Hey, wait!" Marco climbed beside me, looking at the stocky lines of the thing. "Jesus, it's a ghostship!"

Getting to the gangplank notch, I lifted up two more bags to whoever was there and then took Marco's supplies and tossed them up too. When I turned back, he was trying to figure out how to get up there himself.

I pointed back down the ship. "There's a rope ladder back there!"

"Can't you just give me a boost?!"

I withheld a comment and brushed past him to where the rickety contraption swung back and forth, snagging it and putting my boot on the first rung. He crowded in as I started up and I yelled back down at him. "Don't get on this thing until I get all the way off. We don't know if it'll hold two men!"

I climbed the rest of the way, where Roy gave me a hand, ushering me toward a set of doors in the main cabin to our left, the great steam stack encased in ice towering above. You could see where somebody, probably Henry, had forced open one of the doors, knocking away the coating of ice that lay shattered on the deck.

Closing a gloved hand around the handle, I turned it and pushed, stumbling inside.

I shrugged the goggles from my face and scanned the room. It was larger than I would've supposed with a table and chairs to the right and a smaller area to the rear, which I assumed was the captain's quarters. The thing reeked of another period, and in her time she must've been something, but a lot of her outfit and accessories had been pried from the walls in an attempt to salvage, just as I'd suspected.

Jerry and Blackjack were laying out the weapons and supplies on a large table over a scattering of charts, ledgers, and journals in an attempt to see if there was anything else we needed to go back after in the Polar Pig. The bear cub was lying on the table surrounded by a couple of seat cushions, contentedly sleeping away.

Incapable of stopping myself, I yawned. "I think I need a nap too."

Blackjack looked up at me and smiled as Marco stumbled in the door behind, followed by Matty and Roy, who pulled his hood down, revealing his bald head as he threw a darkened canvas bag near an ornate stove that sat in the front of the room. "Coal heat."

I pulled out a chair and sat for a moment. "Good, it must be ten below in this cabin."

"Not for long." He went to the stove and opened it, grabbing a scoop shovel from the stand and shoving the long-dead coals aside. He gestured with a Zippo lighter. "Grab one of those old sea charts from the table and throw it over here?"

I did as the navigator said and then watched as he ripped it up and wadded it in the burner, in the big potbelly stove. "Where's your friend?"

"Henry?" I looked at Blackjack. "Probably getting the lay of the land; seeing if there's anything we can use to help us survive."

"So, we're stuck here."

Marco was already standing by the ice-cold stove attempting

to get warm. I pulled his .357 from my pocket and tossed it on the table. "You're welcome to go take your chances out on the ice."

He smirked a response. "You don't like me, do you?"

"Not especially, no."

There was a jarring at the door as it sprang open and the Cheyenne Nation stepped in, also carrying an identical coal bag. He nodded toward the growing fire. "It would appear we had the same idea."

Matty gestured to the smaller room in the rear. "The captain's quarters has another stove in there, if you want to get it going."

"What if we run out of coal?"

Henry threw the coal bag over his shoulder and lowered his hood and vintage goggles, switching off his headlamp and starting for the aft cabin. "There are only fourteen tons of the stuff below, so we will have to be prudent."

I followed him as Matty pulled a few of the ledgers aside and flipped through the dry paper and called after us. "Did you happen to catch the ship's name?"

I stopped and thought about the words that had been stenciled on the rear of the freighter. "Something Asian I guess—*Baychimo*—but London is her port of call."

His face froze. "What?"

"I know, it sounds funny but—"

"No, the name. Did you say '*Baychimo*'?"

"Yep."

"My God . . ."

"What?"

"The *Ångermanelfven*. She's a Swedish steamer built for the Germans back in 1914 that was given to the British in war reparations and finally used by the Hudson's Bay Company to supply the outposts here and pick up a store of furs in trade with the Inuit and Anglo trappers. But she was deserted by Captain Sidney Cornwell and his crew back on October 15, 1931."

"1931?" Marco laughed. "You've got to be kidding."

"She's a legend." Matty stood, looking around. "She got caught in the big ice and they had to abandon her near Horseshoe Reef. They landed planes and took some passengers and crew away to Nome, while others set up camp to survive the winter in hopes of getting her loose. But she vanished, and everyone thought she must've sunk." He cast a nostalgic gaze around the cabin, even going so far as to run a hand over some of the woodwork. "But she didn't . . . Less than a year later Charlie Adraigailak and Ollie Morris found her off Point Barrow and were able to get out to her on the ice with dogsleds and discovered she was still carrying over a million dollars' worth of exquisite furs—sable; white, black, and silver fox; ermine; beaver; lynx; wolf; and even polar bear pelts."

Roy shook his head. "So, it really is abandoned?"

"A long time ago, yes. A year later she was spotted by Leslie Melvin, a trapper who was sledding near the coast of Herschel Island. Supposedly he got on board and liberated a few bottles of brandy and a Christmas cake."

The navigator perked up. "Wait, there's booze aboard?"

"There were other sightings, and there was a letter found by an Inuit hunting party from Richard Finnie, an explorer who they say left a priceless number of Arctic artifacts on board."

Blackjack nodded. "I have heard these legends myself."

"It was sighted again almost ten years later, during the Second World War, and also in the early sixties by an Inupiat hunting party in kayaks, and even the Distant Early Warning Line of radar stations is said to have picked her up in '65. Not only that, but she was also spotted by locals who were working on a tanker project between Icy Cape and Point Barrow last year . . ."

From the doorway between the captain's quarters and the dining room, I gave him a quizzical look. "How the hell do you know all this stuff?"

Roy shrugged while pulling out a chair. "That's his thing, ghostships."

Marco spoke up. "Great, so there's no way to contact the outside world and let them know where we are?"

Matty moved forward, toward the bridge. "Well, it's not impossible, but the chances that the equipment are still whole and operational . . ."

"Great."

I left the conversation and joined Henry in the captain's quarters, where he'd gotten a fire going, but the smoke was pushing back out of the stove. "Clogged?"

His dark eyes studied the fire. "Probably."

He started to stand but I pushed him back down. "I've been out there getting warm. You stay. I'll go."

He smiled a tight grin. "Be careful."

"What could happen, I fall on the deck and break more ice?"

His eyes went back to the fire. "Possibly more, yes."

I paused for a moment and then left Henry and moved toward the main cabin, buttoning, zipping, tightening, and gloving before announcing to the group, "I'm going to go up there and knock the ice off the stacks to get the captain's stove to draw."

Marco warmed his hands by the stove. "Be sure to tell us if you find a million dollars' worth of furs or valuable antiquities, would you?"

"You bet." Reaching down, I rubbed the cub's belly and felt its warmth as I watched it curl around my fingers, then withdrew my hand and headed out.

The wind had let up a bit outside as I lodged the door shut and flipped on my headlamp, wondering how much battery power the thing had left.

I figured there had to be a route that led to the bridge and was rewarded with an exterior stairwell. It was covered with ice but was still more manageable than the goofy rope ladders, so I gripped the railing and climbed.

The bridge was encased in ice almost a foot thick as I worked my way around on the walk, finally getting to the roof of the quarters. The one stack was smoking happily where the lee side of ice had broken and fallen away, probably from the heat of the fire, but the other one farther back was completely encased.

Peering round, I could see a floating hook on some holders underneath the railing to my left, so I pounded on it until it came loose and I pulled it out. It was a hefty thing with a maple shaft and a brass end. I hated to use it to bang on the ice, but there really weren't any other options.

Straddling the railing, I stepped out onto the roof and tested it to make sure it wouldn't collapse, but as old as the *Baychimo* was, she was a sturdy ghostship.

As I approached the first stack, I couldn't help but wonder how a little steel-hulled freighter like this could've wandered the Arctic Ocean for almost fifty years and not get crushed by the gigantic ice sheets that had destroyed so many others.

From the *Flying Dutchman* of the seventeenth century down, ghostships were reputed to be cursed, but if this trusty little steamer had survived this long, I'd say she was most assuredly charmed.

Reaching the stack while humming the overture from Wagner's *Der fliegende Holländer*, I tapped at a metal cap and then watched as the ice quickly broke apart, falling away to the sounds of the muffled cheering below.

I stepped around the ice, continuing toward the stack in the rear and could plainly see that the sledding was going to be a bit rougher. With so much ice, I wondered how hard I could pound on the structure without knocking it completely off the roof.

I tapped it with a few swings of the hook and wasn't surprised when nothing happened. Rearing back, I gave it a tremendous wallop and watched as the thicker side broke and shed a small piece away. I jammed the point of the hook into the ice and pried until I thought it might break, when it suddenly gave out with a terrible *thunk* and one side broke completely off.

Smoke poured out and there was cheering below, and I tapped away the rest before I lost my grip on the hook and watched it twist around and slide across the roof to where it hung over the edge astern.

Grumbling, I trudged through the snow, carefully crunching through the crust and onto the thick sheen underneath. Slipping a few times, I finally got within reach of the thing and grabbed it, taking the time to look over the side where the C-119 Polar Pig had disappeared beneath the ice and sea—completely gone.

8

SS *BAYCHIMO*, LOCATION UNKNOWN, NORTH SLOPE, ALASKA

DECEMBER 23, 1970

"The Beaufort Gyer. It's this strange oceanographic phenomenon that slowly swirls generally clockwise, about ten times the size of Lake Michigan with chunks of ice in it over thirty miles in circumference, some of them thousands of years old. There's a scientific research station named T3 on one of them; this mammoth ice pan circled around out there for years before it finally slipped free and floated down toward Greenland, where it broke up," Matty explained.

I unbuttoned my parka, the heat in the dining room finally approaching zero as Matty, Henry, and I sat at the table. "So, you're thinking this ship periodically gets trapped in this . . . Beaufort Gyre, and then slips free long enough to get sighted before being pulled back in where it disappears for decades until it appears again?"

Matty shrugged. "What else could it be?"

The Cheyenne Nation grunted.

I glanced around at the sleeping people, piled into all corners of the room, most of them near the roaring stoves that provided a cheery light in the otherwise dismal, frozen surroundings. "Dumb luck?"

"They found rocks and caribou antlers embedded in the ice, as well as the bones of animals that had been extinct for centuries."

I walked over to the cabinets in the mess and began opening and closing them until I found what I was looking for in the form of a half-bottle of Château de Laubade Armagnac, which sat next to a full bottle. Pulling the half-full container from the cabinet, I retrieved a handful of tumblers from the captain's quarters and sat them on the table between Matty, Henry, and me. "Drink?"

"Never touch the stuff."

"Maybe you should start." I shoved a glass in his direction and dumped a little in. "Henry?"

He waved me off.

"More for me." I poured a tumblerful and then picked up the bottle and attempted to read the crumbling French label in the firelight before resting it back on the table amid the supplies, curling ledgers, blueprints, and yellowed charts. "So, what are the chances that this Beaufort Gyre will pull the *Baychimo* back in and swirl us around out there for another ten years?"

Matty's expression turned somber as he nudged his tumbler with his fingertips. "I don't know."

Picking up my glass, I swirled the deep-honey-colored liquid. "How come this thing hasn't been spotted by aircraft, satellites, or other ships?"

"Do you know how big the Arctic is?"

My eyes darted toward Henry, who remained silent, and then back to Matty over the glass. "I concede your point."

"Ninety-five percent of the time the *Baychimo* has probably been covered in snow and ice."

"Why hasn't it sunk?"

He shrugged. "Dumb luck?"

The Bear lifted an empty glass. "Here is to *stupide chance*."

Matty nodded. "Let's hope that we get some ourselves." He took a sip and then slowly lowered the tumbler, all the time studying the tabletop.

"Something bothering you?"

The young man took a moment to respond. "Mike."

I nodded as he got up and walked over to the nearest stove, opening it with the shovel and tossing a few more chunks of coal into the fire. "He was a good guy. Do you actually think a polar got him?"

I stared at the reflection of the fire on the ice-encased windows, thinking about the instant the pilot from Texas had disappeared. "I can't think of what else it could've been."

"But he was unconscious, right?"

Henry spoke. "What difference does it make?"

Matty turned to him. "I'd like to think he wasn't aware he was being eaten alive."

I nodded. "It's possible he was already dead when he hit the ice; that screw attached to the guideline came flying around at a good sixty miles an hour when it hit him."

Henry nodded, a grim look on his face. "*Stupide chance.*"

Matty stared at the fire. "Dumb luck."

I swigged down some more brandy. "Dumb luck."

"Maybe I will have that drink . . ."

I poured the Cheyenne Nation a dollop and he sat and sipped while I turned back to Matty. "So, this inland operations base you were able to make contact with . . . ?"

"I radioed them but didn't receive a response. I mean, there was some static, but that could've been anything." He took his tumbler in hand and then shook his head. "Did you see if anything on the bridge might be operable?"

"No, I figured, what's the use? If the radios operated on battery power or generators, they've been long dead."

He studied the liquid in the glass and then lifted it to his lips, taking a quick swig with an elongated face. "But we've got some batteries we could possibly string together and get them to work if we can figure out how to get a six-volt system to work off twelve-volt batteries."

"You're kidding."

"Nope, I'm a genuine electrical engineer, and if the things are in any way stable on the voice transmission shortwave,

I might be able to get the radio to operate. If not, I'm sure they've got a Morse code system I can probably get working with enough battery power."

"The radios would be on the bridge?"

"Or adjacent to it in a radio room or shack."

Henry looked out the windows, through the ice and darkness. "How long until daylight?"

I pulled out my pocket watch and studied it. "Four hours from now and less than four hours of light to work with— the two most powerful warriors are patience and time."

Matty stared at me. "Are you some kind of scholar or something?"

Henry chuckled as I stood, pulling my sealskin parka back on and buttoning up. "English major."

"You're kidding."

"That's the usual response I get." I nudged the Cheyenne Nation's shoulder. "You coming?"

"Do I have to?"

"No."

"Then I will." He stood, fetching his own parka and gloves from over near the stove in the captain's quarters where Blackjack slept, curled around the bear cub. "May I borrow one of the headlamps? I want to explore belowdecks."

"I thought you already checked down there?"

"No, after finding the coal hold, I walked the entire upper decks and then circled back."

I pulled on my gloves and adjusted my goggles and hat. "See anything?"

"Perhaps."

I stared at him as I fetched one of the remaining head-lamps from the table, along with both of the big revolvers. "What does that mean?"

"It means perhaps."

I handed him both light and force. "Just in case."

We finished bundling up as Matty woke Roy and in-formed him of the plan, all of us figuring it best to have at least one person awake and aware as we prowled around. I took the last two headlamps for Matty and me and then held the other revolver, studying it. "I'd trade every one of these things for a good 12 gauge with lead slugs."

"Or a bazooka." Matty stared at both Henry and me as we stood next to the door. "You really think that bear might've followed us?"

"No, but it seems to me there are always more polars around these parts." I pushed on the door, and we made our way out into the deep freeze. The wind had died down even more, but I figured it would pick back up when the light started to change. I also thought about how we'd only have a little over four hours of sunlight for any kind of rescue op-eration, that is, if the inland operations base or Northstar had reported us missing.

We made our way across the ice-coated ship to stairs lead-ing to the bridge and another set diving down into its bowels.

Henry flipped on his light and continued belowdecks, throwing up a hand knowing full well I was watching him go.

Matty and I turned to the left and continued upward toward the glass box that was the bridge. The ice was thicker on top and, not having my previous experience, Matty slipped and fell, sliding into the railing and toward the twelve-foot fall to his left. I gripped his hood and pulled him back just as I located the door.

After allowing him to get his footing, I thumped an elbow into the ice and watched with relief as it cracked. I gave it another shot and large sections fell away as I tried the lever on the door, which didn't move. Wrestling with it a bit more, I felt something give way as either the lock mechanism opened or broke. I got my answer when I pulled the door open and the inner handle clattered on the metal floor.

The interior of the old freighter's nerve center was a trip back in time, with a wooden stand and a massive brass ship's wheel. There was a freestanding compass in front of it and an indicator that hung overhead along with a few antique-looking headsets, but no radios.

The great windows all around were completely caked with ice, turning them into nothing more than frosted mirrors.

I moved inside and Matty followed, peering around before shuffling to the left and trying another door that was much more compliant.

It swung open, and the light from Matty's headlight revealed a room the size of a broom closet with a panel of radios and a counter where there was an honest-to-goodness Morse telegraph key.

Matty pulled back a chair, slipped a Swiss Army Knife

from his pocket, and began loosening the screws on the panel. As he did that, I walked back into the main room to investigate. There was damage from treasure hunters who had tried to pry more parts from the ghostship, including the brass wheel, where the connecting nut had been battered with something like a hammer to try to break it free.

I thought I saw something passing on the far side of the windows in the bridge, but with it being as dark as it was, I doubted that was possible. Thinking it might be Henry, I crossed to where the partially open door thrummed on its hinges in a Morse code of its own, and I reached for the hole where the latch had been to open it when it slammed shut.

Figuring it was just the wind, I pulled again but it didn't budge. This time I put my weight into it, but once again with negligible results.

I thought there was a strange scuffing noise outside, so I leaned down, placing my ear against the door, and could have sworn I heard some form of labored breathing. "Henry?"

The noise stopped.

"Henry?" Giving the door one last push, I gave up and retreated to the radio room where Matty gestured toward the panels he'd unattached and pulled from the racks, where I could see there were only a few with unbroken tubes.

I pulled my balaclava down and asked, "What can we do?"

Leaving his face covering in place, he pointed to the telegraph key.

"You've got to be kidding."

He shook his head no.

He pulled the one faceplate closest to the tiny transmitter and pointed to where two of the tubes were still intact.

"Can we take it back to the captain's quarters and work on it there?"

He nodded and began disconnecting it from the wiring panel, even going so far as to remove the remaining tubes from the other panels and shoving them into separate pockets.

"The only problem we've got now is that the door we came in through shut and is jammed, and short of shooting it open, I have no idea how we're going to get out—other than breaking a window."

He nodded again, at what I wasn't sure, then collected his supplies and entered the main room before turning left and going over to another door beyond the helm. He gestured toward the door and I turned the handle, opening it into another stairwell that led down from the inside.

I gestured for him to go first and then gave one last glance at the stuck door, wondering what exactly I'd heard on the other side before I followed Matty.

Tromping down the metal steps behind him, I felt relief there wasn't any ice, even though it was as dark as the inside of a cow. At a landing, I moved past Matty and opened a door to some sort of upper control room for the engine below. The main stack ran through the room and I could see another doorway to the right. I opened it, finding myself in a narrow hallway that I figured must've connected to the mess.

Moving to the left, I opened another hatch and happily

found myself in the much warmer dining room where we'd started out.

I ushered Matty inside, closed the hatch behind us, pulled down my face covering, and lifted my goggles and nudged my hat back, noticing for the first time that I couldn't see my breath. "It's downright balmy in here."

I moved some things, including a flare gun and an assortment of hand flares I hadn't seen, and watched as Matty carefully placed the parts of the antiquated equipment on the table.

"I can't believe we're relying on Wells Fargo technology."

Dropping his hood, he peeled off his goggles and lowered his balaclava. "Western Union, please."

I shook my head and threw some more coal in the two stoves, watching as a sleeper, as well as the bear cub, rolled over. "If, and I say *if*, we get that thing going, will anybody be listening?"

"Wireless sets were required from 1912 on, and ever since the sinking of the *Titanic* there's been an international agreement that all ships would have a twenty-four-hour distress-signal receiver. So, as long as we can get a signal out on this frequency, we should be able to reach somebody."

"How's your Morse code, hippie?"

He sat about arranging the tubes from his pockets and then pulled off his parka and sat in a chair. "Rough, but back in San Diego Bay they made us learn this stuff . . ." He smiled at me through long hair. "And right now, I'm pretty glad they did."

"If, and once again I mean *if*, you get this thing going—it's going to have to go back up on the bridge and get reconnected?"

"Yes."

I nodded and scanned the room at the sleeping bodies, not seeing the navigator. "Where's Roy?"

Matty shrugged. "Maybe he went back to sleep?"

"With Henry gone, there are only three people in here, Blackjack, Jerry, and Marco." I studied the wrapped and snoring lumps on the floor. "We got him up and Roy was sitting over there." I pointed to the empty chair near the hatch that led to the outside deck. "He looked like he was going to fall back asleep, but he was sitting right there with his parka as a blanket."

Preoccupied with the radio parts, Matty waved a hand at me. "Maybe he's sleeping in another part of the room."

I did a quick circle and came back to the table. "He's not here."

"Then I guess he went out; maybe he had to go to the bathroom or something."

I stared at the door, thinking of the sounds I'd heard. "I'm going to go out and look around, just to make sure he didn't fall and hurt himself or something."

Matty nodded and I suited up, going over to the door and patting my right pocket to make sure the .44 was still there. "Try and get that thing operable so that we can do the outside work in the daylight, however much we get."

He nodded. "Roger that."

I adjusted my goggles and switched on the headlamp, then forced open the door, stepping out and into the darkness. I couldn't see any fresh prints in the rippling snow, but it was possible that the wind had erased any.

Where would the navigator have gone? Maybe Matty was right and he'd just gone out to see a man about a horse, but where was he now? If I were a toilet, where would I be?

Rather than following the same route, I took a right and trudged back toward the aft to check the door along the main cabin. It opened easily and turned out to be the bathroom, but it was empty. I walked back toward the open railings and the single scow that hung over the forward cargo hatch, then examined the flat-bottomed dinghy. I figured we could all get in there if things got bad enough, load it with ourselves and our supplies, and take what little chance we had in an open boat on the Arctic Ocean.

In a blizzard.

Or maybe not.

I continued across the poop deck and around an elevated set of doors that could possibly lead to the coal stores. When I got to the transom, I peered over the edge. I'm not sure what I thought I was going to find there. Perhaps that the plane had resurfaced? But to my disappointment, the ice had resettled and the snow had covered its surface as if the Polar Pig never existed.

I gave up and crossed around the main cabin to the other side of the ship where there was another gangway notch in the bulwark but little else.

Trudging in that direction, I wondered what had happened to Henry let alone Roy as I got to the other side of the bridge and looked down, where an accommodation ladder lay on the snow below.

It was strange. The thing wasn't covered in snow, as if it had fallen only recently. I ran my headlamp along the side of the hull and could see that the majority of the snow had been knocked away.

I aimed my lamp downward to examine the area where I stood and could see that the snow was flattened, as if something had been rolled around on the deck—or something had climbed on or off?

Had Roy or Henry tried to climb down the ladder and it collapsed? If they had, they were still down there, because it was a good twelve feet—much higher than a human could climb. I decided to traverse to the other side and use the rope ladder to get down on the ice so I could at least check it out.

I started around the front of the bridge when I felt an uneven quality to the snow on the deck and stopped. Again, readjusting my headlamp, I ducked my head and noticed that my boot was sitting in a deep depression in the snow.

I knelt, placing my hand in the hollow that was more than twice as wide as my outstretched fingers, at least eighteen inches, and almost three times as long—with five distinct claw marks the size of paring knives.

Bear.

A very, very large bear.

9

DECEMBER 23, 1970

I am a large man, but at the moment I didn't particularly feel like it.

I closed my fingers around the Smith & Wesson revolver in my parka and quietly drew it while turning off the headlamp with my other hand. I didn't think there was reason to advertise my location any more than necessary, but I also knew that bears hunt mostly by smell, which wasn't helping to settle my nerves. In the darkness, I immediately wanted to turn my headlight back on and look for boot prints, but I didn't think that was such a great idea.

I stood and placed my back against the metal wall of the bridge, listening for any signs, but all I could hear was the wind and the constant groan of the ice against the steel hull of the ship.

If Roy heard something like I did on the flying bridge but, unlike me, was able to get his door open, then I had a pretty good idea what happened to him.

And what about Henry?

I hadn't heard or seen him since he'd headed down below-decks. It was unlikely that the monster we saw could fit down there, but the Cheyenne Nation would've had to come back sometime.

Maybe the tracks were old, but what about the ladder and the snow that had been swiped away?

I took a deep breath and considered that the first thing to do was get word back to the others in the living quarters that there was a bear out here. It couldn't be the bear that we'd seen out on the ice—the one that had taken Mike—or at least I didn't think so.

If it was just a curious bear that happened to stumble onto the *Baychimo* the same as us, it was likely that he'd climbed on, gotten bored, and then wandered off. But if that were the case, then where were Roy and Henry?

It was hard for me to believe that someone as capable as the Cheyenne Nation could've been taken, but I supposed all things were possible.

I tried not to think about that.

I was going to have to wake Blackjack up and get her thoughts on the subject, seeing as how she probably knew more about polars than I did.

Sliding along the wall, I kept the .44 out in front of me and wished once again for a shotgun, among other things.

There was a noise to my right, and I figured it was time to think about where I'd go if I made it around the bridge and was confronted with the largest land carnivore on the planet. I could always run back this way or leap down for the hatch covers amidships, but whatever I did, he'd catch me. My only hope was to find an area he couldn't climb into, somewhere that the limited space of the metal hatchways would hold him off.

I glanced around the corner and nothing was there, at least as near as I could see without my headlamp. Or maybe the wind had gotten the ladder and the snow on the far side and the print was just an old one.

Taking another deep breath, I continued along the wall until I got to the hatch that led to the living quarters and turned the lever and stepped inside. I tipped back my hat, lowered my hood, and took off my goggles, and I found Matty working on the radio set and Roy seated on the chair where we'd left him before. I shook my head at the navigator as I pulled my face covering down. "Where the hell were you?"

He looked up at me, confused. "What?"

"Before, when we came back, where the hell were you?"

He adjusted his glasses. "My stomach's been acting up so I went to the bathroom, it's right out there . . ."

"I know where it is, I've been out there wandering around trying to find you and saw fresh bear tracks."

He sat up a little straighter. "What?"

"A bear, a very big one."

"I didn't see anything."

I fell back on the old maxim. "Doesn't mean it didn't see you." I checked the room once more. "Has anybody seen Henry?"

"The big Indian?"

"Yep."

He shot a glance at Matty. "No, is he missing?"

The radioman lifted his gaze for an instant before returning to his work. "He went out with us, but didn't he say he was going belowdecks to have a look around?"

I walked over to the stove and peeled off my gloves to warm my hands. "He should've been back by now."

"Maybe he found something interesting."

"Or maybe something found him." I began the process of suiting back up. "I'm going out to find him."

Matty raised his eyes. "How long until daylight?"

"About three hours." I pointed at the pile of parts that was starting to resemble an Erector set. "That thing going to be ready?"

I watched as he pulled a poker from the fire with a gloved hand and connected two pieces by remelting some solder. "I think so."

I moved toward the table. "Do we have anything else I can use if I run into that thing out there?"

They both looked at me, Roy being the first to speak. "There are some flares, but that's it."

Blackjack appeared in the opening between the rooms. "Take some of those hand flares. They've got friction ignitors."

I grabbed up the M16, stuffed it under my arm, and picked up a few of the flares to inspect them. "What good are these going to be?"

Loosening her parka, she gestured toward the flares. "All animals are afraid of fire—they might not recognize that M16 as a threat, but fire they will. Besides, if you're going down in the hold, it'd be nice to have a light source if the batteries die on that headlamp."

She had a point, so I picked up a half dozen of the things and crammed them into my pockets. "You just pull the caps?"

Roy nodded. "Yeah."

I pointed a gloved finger at him. "Nobody goes out till I get back, clear?"

I dumped out the coal bucket and sat it by the door. "If you have to go, go in this. Got it?"

All three nodded. I turned the lever for the door and stepped out, closing it behind me. Deciding I was likely to walk off the ship unless I turned my headlamp on, I erred on the side of caution and clicked on the light. I figured I'd track Henry's trail, so I followed the trampled snow to the bridge, descending the stairwell where I'd watched him disappear.

I turned the corner, took the stairs, and was happy to find a somewhat confined area.

There was a set of doors there and I noticed that one of them was slightly open. Pulling it aside, I looked in the lower hold near the centerline bulkhead, a vast, open space roughly the size of a ballroom with hard hatch covers above. "There's no way a bear could get down here."

Water had leaked in from above, and the effect of all the icy stalactites gave the impression you were in a massive Arctic cave. There were canvas covers thrown over a majority of the space. I had other things to find in the meantime but couldn't help but wonder what cargo the old girl was carrying.

I followed a metal gangway and crossed to starboard where I found another stairwell that led deeper to stowage in holds near the tank top.

There was a silting of snow on the metal grating, and I could see Henry's boot prints leading forward but none coming back. With as many entryways and exits as there were on the old freighter, it wasn't surprising that he might've taken another way to return—but what was taking him so long?

Moving down the walkway with the mouse gun in the lead, I stopped and swiveled my head to the other side of the hold but the headlamp would only illuminate so much. I thought I could see some kind of movement in the shadows, so I pulled down my balaclava and spoke. "Henry?"

Nothing.

I raised my voice. "Henry!"

Still nothing.

Thumbing my face cover up to afford a little more protection, I continued down the walkway along the tween deck centerline bulkhead where a few of the hatches hung open, and I peered in those rooms. A few were extra living quarters and others were ship's storage.

I moved past the main centerline bulkhead that divided the ship, and through the feeble headlamp beam I could see another hatch that hung from a single hinge, with pitch black beyond.

I could've sworn I'd seen movement in the darkness, just a bit of something reflected in the beam of my headlamp. I started to take a step toward it when there was a seismic shudder. It felt like something had shifted on one of the connected gangways, the metal echoing through the ship.

I stood there for a moment listening to the silence, then took another step until I was only about six feet from the hatchway, the M16 pointed into the darkness. "Henry?"

Then something flashed through the opening so fast I couldn't tell what it was—all I saw were black lips and gums, strings of slobber, and massive snapping jaws that looked like they belonged on the scoop of a steam shovel.

I stumbled backward and crashed onto the metal gangway as the head of the thing disappeared and a giant claw thrashed out onto the steel mesh of the floor between my legs before swiping at the air above me and then silently drawing back into the darkness.

I lay there with my goggles sideways on my head, trying to be sure that what I saw was what I thought I'd seen. Lowering the goggles I picked up my hat and reset my headlamp. I sat up on my elbows and saw glossy strings of liquid that now strung across the front of my parka, confirming that it—whatever it was—was actually there and was very, very close.

My shaking hands were still pointed at the hatchway, the unfired rifle still there.

Then I remembered the flares in my pocket, so I took one out and pulled the cap, watching it burst into flame, and tossed it through the hatchway.

Nothing.

I stood up, trying to collect my wits and listen, but there was still nothing but the sound of the sizzling flare.

I looked into the next cargo hold and saw the red light illuminating the walkway and more tween-deck hatchways, and then dark, open space.

I'd just started to take a step forward when the same flash of movement thrust through the hatch and knocked me to one side as I hung on to the railing to keep from falling into the lower hold. "Son of a—"

The arm of the thing withdrew again and I couldn't believe the size of it, easily as large as my torso. The other thing I noticed was that part of its hair had been burned away, with scarred skin covering one whole muscled side as it disappeared again.

There had been no sound.

Nothing.

I watched as the flare, only twelve feet away, continued to burn on the gangway inside and could see dark stains in the mesh, and all I could think about was my friend. "Henry!"

Holding on to the railing, I tugged my hat back and leaned to one side to get a better view but the red light from the flare continued to hiss, illuminating only the gangway as if it led into an abyss. "Henry!"

Not wanting to approach the hatchway without further preparation, I quickly scanned for another opening but couldn't see one. I knew the monster could get above decks, but how could he have gotten down in the other hold? Perhaps by prying up the hatches to get inside? If that was the case, then the hold in front of me was the only one he could get into.

I leaned back and scanned the tween-deck rooms to my left and could see a singular hatchway leading into the next hold, past the centerline bulkhead.

I stepped toward it, figuring if the configuration in that hold were similar to this one, then there was no way the polar could get in there either.

I attempted to spin the large wheel and open the hatch with one hand, but it wouldn't budge. I carefully placed the rifle under my arm, braced both hands, and began turning it bit by bit. It grew looser and spun a little more freely until finally there was a clunking sound as it opened about a quarter of an inch.

Staring at the thing with more than a little trepidation, I pointed the M16 toward the hatch and pulled it open slowly.

There were crates in the next room but they weren't stacked very high, and I saw another hatchway to my right that must've opened into the main cargo hold because I could see the flare continuing to glow red on the walkway.

The hatch was too small for the polar to get in there, but that didn't mean there wasn't another way for him to get in.

Carefully pushing the door open the rest of the way, I felt the metal hatchway strike one of the crates and stop. As I panned my headlamp around, it appeared as if this room hadn't been ransacked like the others.

Pushing my way in, I gauged the distance to the door at about twelve feet and figured there was no way that thing could get at me.

The flare continued to burn and I thought about what Blackjack said about how all animals fear fire, and if my observations were correct, either this polar was diseased or had been in some kind of fire that resulted in the disfigurement I'd witnessed.

Maybe the flare was keeping it from the doorway, but the only way to find out was to get closer for a look-see.

All I could think about was how fast and silent the big ambush predator had been and how the hatchways weren't that very different from the holes in the ice that bears like this have been pulling bloody seals from for a hundred and fifty thousand years.

Still keeping my distance, I had to get a bit closer to squeeze around the crates. As near as I could tell, I wasn't making any noise, but I had also thought that earlier when he tried to snatch me through the hatchway.

Easing in front of the crate, I directed the headlamp into the main cargo area, walking through to the other side and slipping around the corner. There was no movement from the opening, and the flare lay there burning like a birthday cake.

If I was serious about finding Henry I was going to have to take a peek inside, but I couldn't say the notion appealed to me.

I took a deep breath and lifted the barrel of the M16, moving toward the door and drifting to the left so I might be able to see the doorway where I'd thrown the flare and where the unwelcoming monstrosity had been loitering.

The flare cast its red light against the steel bulkhead where the door hung but on nothing else. Maybe the thing, having failed at getting me, had climbed back out of the hold above decks where he'd gone his merry way.

I stepped closer, moving now to the right and shining the beam out into the main hold, but I still saw nothing. It was like shining a light into ink.

I took another deep breath and stepped forward again, now within reach of the thing's arm—if it were still there. Drifting farther to the right, I could see something lying on the gangway past the flare.

It was something slim and light-colored with a strap— Henry's bone-framed vintage snow goggles.

I stumbled forward before catching myself. Standing there a few seconds more, I inched closer, searching in every direction in the darkness of the cargo hold before noticing a broken piece of crating that must've been ripped from one of the wooden boxes. I picked it up in my left hand and crouched a little closer to the doorway.

I scanned around to make sure the bear hadn't taken up the position he had at the other hatchway. I couldn't see anything, which was less than reassuring, as I poked the piece of the crate through the doorway, fully expecting to be dragged through by the horrific arm.

When nothing happened, I reached across, working the sharp edge under the strap and lifting. The strap slid up the wood a bit and then stuck as I drew it back toward me.

Then teeth.

From seemingly out of the blackness, giant rows of teeth lodged themselves through the two bars of the railing on the other side of the gangway, the creature's massive head unable to get through.

The bars, each about two inches in diameter, squealed as the bear tried to force its way through to me, the great jaws snapping as I fell back, watching a claw rise and tear at the railing.

I scrambled backward into the crate behind me and sat there trying to force my heart back out of my throat. I then lifted the rifle, pulled the trigger, and heard nothing. I pulled the trigger again, but the weapon had chosen this exact time to freeze.

I continued the futile effort of pulling the trigger and thought about how handy having a rifle rod or assorted tools might be, sighting over the useless weapon as I watched the claws and snout disappear from the light of the flare until the only thing visible was the red reflection in the single malignant eye. We stared at each other in the hiss of the flare, and I noted again the absolute quiet of his attack.

The eye stayed like that and then slowly withdrew just outside the illumination of the flare.

I reached out and again lifted the piece of crating until the goggles slid into my hands. I studied the narrow slit in the caribou antler with blood smeared on one side.

I'd just started to sit up when I heard a noise coming from the doorway.

I raised the M16 and aimed it into the darkness as I heard the very faint noise again—a voice I recognized.

"Walt . . ."

10

"Henry, can you hear me?" His voice had gone silent again. "I know you're there—I heard you."

I tried to angle myself so that I could throw my voice to the left and toward the bow cargo area from where I was sure his voice had come. "Henry!"

His voice was weak. "I can hear you . . ."

"Where the hell are you?"

I listened and could even hear him swallow. "I am in the cargo area next to you."

I checked the wall but couldn't find a hatch there. "Can you see the light from the flare I threw?"

"Yes."

"Are you hurt?"

"Yes."

"How bad?"

There was no answer.

"You get tagged by that bear?"

"Yes."

I stood and walked over to the steel bulkhead, now figuring that the closer I was to him the better chance I had of not only hearing him but having him hear me. "He almost got me about three times." Leaning there, I continued to try to figure out a way of getting to him, but the bulkhead was solid steel with giant rivets holding it in place. "There doesn't seem to be any break in this wall."

"Trust me, there is not."

I knelt down to where his voice seemed to emanate. "I'll have to go above to the main deck and see if I can find a hatch or something . . . Can you see anything?"

"No, my headlamp is dead." He chuckled. "Why not just stroll out on the gangway and come on over."

"What do you think is the story with that monster?"

"This is only a hypothesis, but I have had plenty of time to think about it. I would imagine he has been using this ship as shelter and a point of ambush for quite some time. This bear is malformed and at one time he must have been burned." He coughed and then cleared his throat. "Before he struck, I was able to get in here and I saw a burned section of the aft cargo areas that held coal tonnage, which must have caught fire at one point, possibly when he was onboard."

"Strange behavior, don't you think?"

"Certainly, but it is possible this was the only way he could survive."

"He's big as a house."

"Yes, and maimed as this bear is, he may not be able to swim or he lacks the fur covering a large portion of his body so that he cannot stay warm out on the ice for very long."

"What about the female we found and Wormy . . . and Mike?"

"He may venture out when he has to, but I would say the majority of the time he stays here and waits."

A grim thought. "Where are you hurt?"

"He caught my back as I ran—I think I used to be faster."

"Seriously, your wounds, how bad are they?"

"Seriously bad. I do not have a light to see, but there is a lot of blood."

"Pain?"

"No thanks, I have plenty."

"Funny guy." I stood. "All right, I'm going to go above to try to find a hatch in the deck, or worse yet a porthole or an opening in the hull. What do you need right now other than bandages?"

"Water would be nice. Perhaps something to eat?"

"How are you staying warm?"

"The immersion suit seems to be working well, and I also have about a million dollars' worth of hides in here."

"What?"

I could hear him readjust himself against the plate steel.

"The forward cargo areas are completely full of some of the finest and luxurious hides I have ever seen, thousands of them. At this moment I am completely covered in sable, wolverine, seal, and polar bear furs like a proverbial bug in a rug."

"How nice for you; try not to end up on the inside of that big one just outside the door, would you?"

"I intend not to."

"And try not to bleed too much on the furs. They might be valuable."

"Roger that."

"I'll find a way to get at you, buddy." I took a deep breath, forcing the emotion from my voice. "Worse comes to worse I'll collect that .416 Rigby from Blackjack and be back down here."

"I will patiently await your arrival." I listened as he moved again. "Walt, one more thing . . ."

"What's that?"

"This creature, he can obviously move easily above and belowdecks."

I thought of the paw print near the bridge. "I'll be careful."

"Please do."

I started to walk away but stopped and leaned back, placing a hand on the metal wall. "One thing puzzles me . . ."

He laughed and then coughed again. "What is that?"

"If this polar killed Wormy, that sow bear, and Mike?"

"Yes?"

"Why? I mean, it isn't like he was hungry . . . Why would he kill all of them?

There was a pause before he responded. "Because he enjoys it."

I tried to blame the shiver that ran up my spine on the cold, but I knew that wasn't completely it. "I'll be back, and next time I'll have a weapon that works."

Henry didn't respond, so I crossed the room around the crate toward the inner hatchway, then glanced out at the still-burning flare and the darkness. "You hear me, too, you damned bear? I'll be back."

There was, predictably, no response.

I went through the hatchway and crossed the mostly empty cargo area where I'd come through, stepping out onto the gangway and looking back through the open hatch, still hanging by its one hinge.

Do these flares burn forever, or was time passing slowly for me as my best friend in the world lay mortally wounded, seemingly forever away?

I got to the bridge stairway and began climbing. When I reached the main deck, I was surprised to see an orange glimmer on the horizon like a frying egg yolk.

As I got ready to venture out into the open, I couldn't help but remember how quick the monster had been in striking silently and seemingly out of nowhere. Pulling the .44 from inside my parka, I stepped out onto the main deck and got my bearings, feeling a little reassured by being out of the claustrophobic cargo area and seeing at least a little bit of sun.

I walked forward and scanned the ice-coated railings, then above me toward the flying bridge and the signal mast. There was nothing there as near as I could tell, so I edged my way around the bridge toward the living quarters to see the one lifeboat-like scow swaying on the heavy cables.

I got to the door and pulled the latch, stepping into the luxurious warmth of the two stoves. The entire group was up and moving around as I tipped back my hat, lowered my goggles and poked the balaclava below my chin. "I found Henry."

Matty lifted his eyes from the radio he was repairing, which now seemed to be in working order. "Good."

"No, not good."

Blackjack came up beside me. "Something has happened?"

"He's trapped belowdecks, and there's a monster bear out there." They all stared at me. "I'm not kidding."

Jerry shook his head, holding the bandage there. "Another one?"

Marco backed away from the stove till he stood against the wall. "It's that same fucking bear."

"Most likely." I unbuttoned my parka and tossed the useless M16 on the table along with all the flares in my pockets. "It would appear we are trespassing on this ship; this bear seems to have taken up residency here, possibly for years."

Jerry began dissembling the M16 as Roy had a dejected expression on his face. "Yeah, but Wormy and Mike . . ."

"It leaves when it can and when it has to, but in the meantime, we've unintendedly provided it with room service."

Marco barked a laugh. "Oh, for fuck's sake."

I ignored him and addressed the others. "That M16 is frozen up, but I need some water, food, and bandages for Henry if we can find some." As the others began gathering supplies into a satchel, I leaned over the radioman to admire his work. "How's the ship to shore?"

Mattingly shrugged, pushing out his chair. "I think it'll work if anybody is listening. These batteries are a lot smaller than the ones from the ship, but they're more powerful and might be enough to get a signal out to that inland operations base I was in contact with."

"SOS?"

He smiled. "You got it."

"We're going to have to carry all this stuff back to the radio room?"

He reached for his parka hanging off the back of his chair. "I'm afraid so."

I faced the group. "I'll help him carry these things to the bridge, but then I'm going to get supplies to Henry. He's trapped in one of the forward cargo spaces, meaning you have to get past that bear to get to him . . ."

"It's on this ship now?"

I turned to Marco. "Have you not been listening?" I addressed the others. "I'm going to see if there's a hatch on the main deck or in the hull—some way to get supplies to him—and then figure out a way to get him out of there. In the meantime, I think you should all stay in here and out of sight. I don't think the bear can get in these hatchways, as big as he is, but his head and his claws can, so stay away from doors and windows." I turned back to Matty as we zipped up and adjusted our hoods and goggles. "Blackjack was right, the gun didn't have much of an effect, but he's been burned before and didn't like the flares."

He nodded. "Let's take some."

After I shrugged on the satchel of a canteen, MREs, and supplies for Henry, I scooped up a few flares and deposited them in my pockets and tucked my portion of the radio equipment under one arm. I also grabbed my .45 and put it in one pocket of my parka before patting the big Smith & Wesson .44, making sure it was still stuffed in another pocket.

Blackjack, holding the still-sleeping bear cub, motioned toward her rifle now also lying on the table. "Take mine."

I picked it up and I felt the weight of the thing. "You sure?"

She smiled. "It will do more than those popguns."

"It's kind of close combat out there."

She nodded. "Maybe you can put some distance between you."

Gesturing with the rifle, I nodded and continued toward the door with Matty following. "You gonna be warm enough, staying in the radio shack?"

He adjusted the rest of the equipment that he carried in his arm. "I'll be fine. You're the one who's been out here running around in the cold."

"And I've got some more to do." I tucked the rifle under my arm, turned the door's handle, and pushed it open, popping my head out to check both ways. Stepping onto the deck, I surveyed the area and then motioned for him to follow.

Once outside, Matty responded to the growing sunrise much the same way as I had. "I've never been so happy to see the sun in my life."

I smiled, trudged left toward the stairwell, and turned my head back toward him. "Be careful, I found prints from that bear up here."

I felt better when we got inside the stairwell, and I nosed the barrel of the big Rigby topside before following it out and onto the walkway surrounding the flying bridge. After clearing the area, I motioned for Matty to come up and watched as he opened the door to the bridge and went in. I followed and rested the equipment I was carrying on the counter before backing out and looking at the thick coating of ice on the windows. "I'm going back out to try and get the supplies to Henry while you try and get that thing going."

He nodded, preoccupied.

"You don't even open that door until I get back, okay?"

"Yeah."

I returned to the hatch and pushed it open with my foot, stepping outside with the satchel and the high-powered rifle.

The sun was still peeking between the ironclad clouds, its

rays reflecting on the ice with a sideways light that illuminated half of everything, and if I hadn't been fearing for my
life I would've thought was mesmerizing.

I could now see the entire length of the steamer and the
thick ice that coated it like frosting on a gigantic steel cake.
There was a deckhouse about halfway to the prow of the
ship along with a heavy-lift rig and a mast top and platform.
The rigging was missing or had fallen away, but the decks
appeared solid, as did the hatchways.

I tried to measure the distance I'd gone belowdecks to ap-
proximate where exactly Henry would be. Scoping the rifle,
I swept up the decks past midships where the bulkhead
would be below and could see a lower section of the deck
and the forecastle break. The main hatches were there, but
I was sure they would lead down into the main cargo area
and not where Henry was. There were some openings in the
deck along the side, but I was pretty sure they were just
scuppers; besides, they were clogged with ice.

I studied the deck through the high-powered scope and
could see a few spots where it was exposed—and wooden.

Wooden.

I crossed the walkway and continued down the ice-covered
steps to the main deck, shrugging the strap of the satchel
full of supplies on my shoulder and keeping a wary eye out.

The hatches appeared to be solid and secure, and I couldn't
help but wonder where the behemoth was going in and out.

I moved around the mast platform toward the decking
and could see no hatches or ways of getting to the smaller

cargo area where Henry could be. Kneeling, I examined the grain of the oak planking, grayed by time and wear.

I figured I'd start at the mast platform. I found the doorway leading inside, but what I wanted was hanging on the outside underneath a life preserver with the fading stencil SS BAYCHIMO still legible and the credit for the Lindholmen shipyard in Sweden and the rights for building the little ship. I snatched the masting axe and pulled it loose, watching the ice fall away from the broad metal head and hickory handle that looked like a tool from the Middle Ages.

The thing was heavy as I popped it on my shoulder and walked to the wooden area I'd seen through the scope, then pushed away the snow, carefully resting the satchel and the rifle on the deck. I looked at the railing of the hull and then back to the distance to the centerline bulkhead, then raised the axe and with a mighty swing drove it into the wood, where it bounced off with a tremendous clatter—barely leaving a dent.

I stared at the tiny divot in the wood in disbelief. "You've got to be kidding me."

I raised it again and I brought it down with another swing. A more substantial break in the surface, the fresh wood revealed underneath. Raising the axe again and again, I was finally making a reasonable amount of headway before suddenly breaking through the four-inch decking and into the darkness below.

With a few more whacks, I'd opened a sliver of space about two inches wide and a foot long but noticed a metal bracing at both ends. I knelt down and yelled in the hole. "Are you there?!"

Henry's voice was weak, but it was there. "I am . . ."

Standing to redouble my efforts, I began breaking away chunks of the wood and soon discovered there was a heavy metal framework under it. After breaking more away, I came to the conclusion that the openings were only about 10 × 12 inches in whole.

I squinted around in the increasing light and knelt back down again, grabbing the canteen out of the satchel and lowering by the strap through the hole. "Can you see this?"

"Yes."

I pushed my arm through and lowered the canteen even more. "Can you reach it?"

"No."

"If I drop it, where will it land?"

"At my feet."

An unsettling thought raced across my mind as I pressed the side of my face against the deck. "Henry, can you stand up?"

"At the moment, no."

"What do you mean, 'at the moment'?"

"I have not tried, but I think there is damage to my back."

"Here, take this water." I dropped it and then grabbed the satchel and pushed it through the hole and dangled it by the strap from the length of my arm. "Can you see this?"

I listened as he drank and then spoke. "Yes."

"It's some MREs and bandages."

"Just drop it."

I did and then retrieved my arm, sticking my face in the hole. "We got the radio working, or at least a ship-to-shore telegraph key."

He chuckled.

"Don't laugh, it's all we've got the power for. Matty's in the radio shack signaling out right now . . . Have you seen the bear?"

"Not lately, no."

"Maybe he wandered off." I pushed up my hat and goggles and could feel the warmth of the sun striking the side of my face. "Have something to eat and drink and I'll circle back around and see about getting you out of there." I started to go but then yelled down. "Do you still have your pistol?"

"No, it's out there on the gangway."

"Hell."

I sat up and I closed my eyes, tipping my hat back and letting the sun's rays warm me, only to have something block them. After a few seconds, I opened my eyes to see, on the other side of the main hatches, standing erect on two feet, backlit by the sun and peering down at me, the towering silhouette of a fourteen-foot polar bear.

11

Neither of us moved.

There was a good forty feet between us, and I figured the hatches could surely hold his weight, which I estimated to be approaching three thousand pounds. Staring into the sun like I was, I could see only the bear's outline, black with the orange glow behind him. He was misshapen on one side, which amplified his monstrous proportions.

I slipped my eyes to the right and could see the barrel of the Rigby just within reach but seemingly very far away. And likewise for the two pistols inside my parka—an impossible distance away given the brief moment in which I had to act.

I curled my left hand around the shaft of the masting axe,

but I was aware that in the current situation it would be about as useful as a pen knife in an artillery fight.

The only cover would be the mast platform to my right, but that was a good twenty feet away. Do I throw the axe, grab the rifle, and get off a shot before trying to reach the metal three-story cabin?

There were windows in the third story but only portholes in the lower one. The question was, Could I get the door open?

The bear leaned to one side, then sniffed the air between us.

Playing a hand out toward the rifle, I watched him lean again, perhaps moving his shadow so as to get a better look at me. I stopped moving and froze there, staring back at him.

His head dropped a bit, then moved back and forth as if he couldn't see me with his one eye, or at least wasn't sure.

"Walt?" Henry's voice had come through the hole in the deck.

Gently, I shushed him.

His voice rose up again, and there were some scraping noises from below. "What is going on?"

I hissed. "Will you be quiet, he's up here."

The bear focused more directly on me and slowly began lowering himself down on all fours, the position he was going to have to take if he were to charge.

"I may have to run for it."

"Run, I can climb up on one of the crates and distract

him." Suddenly, Henry's hand, covered in blood, appeared from the hole in the deck. "He will smell the blood and come for me."

The bear was now down on all fours, his front paws resting on the main hatch cover, now sniffing with a greater purpose.

"Where did all that blood come from?"

Henry's voice rose again, and the answer chilled me more than the bear. "Me."

The monster lunged forward. I figured throwing the axe was stupid given I might need every weapon I could get my hands on in the next few moments, so instead I rolled to the right, picked up the rifle, and threw myself toward the mast platform with weapons in both hands.

The bear turned toward me, confused, but Henry was yelling and the smell of blood was more than the giant could ignore as he veered toward Henry's bloody hand waving from the deck.

I just hoped the Cheyenne Nation would get his hand back down before the creature got there as I stumbled up the first three steps of the platform and turned the corner to find the hatchway door hanging open.

I threw myself inside and slammed the door shut with my boots as the beast attempted to get in the short entryway, hammering at the hatch, throwing it back at me, and shoving me across the floor.

A great claw swept inside, but as soon as it attempted to withdraw I leapt with the masting axe and buried it in the bear's foreleg. The arm withdrew, and dropping the axe, I slammed my shoulder into the hatch, spinning the wheel, which effectively locked it as long as it held.

I stood there in the center of the room, shaking from the adrenaline among other things, and listened as the creature pounded on the door but still didn't make a single sound.

I checked around the room to make sure there wasn't another way in, and saw only more storage crates, piles of cable, assorted hooks, and hardware. There was a stairwell leading above, so I picked up the rifle and started that way when a shadow passed by one of the portholes.

Standing still, I watched as it passed another before circling the platform and searching for a way in. I got to the steps and carefully started up, attempting to not make a sound.

There was a second floor but there were no windows. I climbed to the third, which was completely surrounded by glass, the majority covered in inches of ice. On the lee side there was less, and over the control panel for the heavy-rig system I was able to see past the swinging scow and down to the hole I'd chopped into the deck, thankfully noting a lack of bloodstained, disembodied hands.

I then saw the bear limping on the front paw I'd hacked, but it didn't seem to have impaired him much as he continued to circle the platform, searching for a way in.

I turned back toward the flying bridge, hoping that Matty was getting through, but then swiveled to face the bear, only to see he was staring directly at me.

I watched as he lumbered up and placed the paw I'd buried the axe into against the platform wall and stood, his head almost as high as the floor of the third level where I was.

I could see his head clearly, the horrific scarred side of his face with part of his left jaw exposed, an ear missing, and the eye a piggish orb glowing with malice.

If I could get one of the windows open, I might be able to plant a bullet in his broad head. My thought was interrupted when he got a paw on a railing and lifted himself up, rising another six feet and reaching a forepaw just short of the glass between us.

I backed away, thinking about how many rounds I could get into him in short order and whether it would be enough.

His big paws thumped against the metal sides of the platform, cracking the glass as the claws scraped for purchase as he silently considered how to get at me.

"Hey, Walt!"

I looked down at the hole in the deck thinking it must've been Henry calling me, but then I heard it again from behind.

"Walt!"

Matty.

I made my way around the winch-operating controls but couldn't see anything through the ice that covered the window. Rearing back, I smashed the thing with the axe, watching the shards of glass and ice fall away as Matty waved at the railing of the bridge.

"What are you doing?"

I yelled at the top of my lungs. "Bear! The bear is out there!"

He froze, but then I saw his attention shift to the base of the platform.

I leaned forward to see what he was looking at: the monster standing under the winch boom near the main hatch covers, its focus completely on the radioman standing at the railing.

"Get back inside! Get back inside!" I dropped the axe and I pulled the .416 to my eye, flipping up the rubber lens covers on the scope, aiming the high-powered rifle.

And found nothing.

Scanning the deck with the scope, I finally lowered it and hung out the window, sweeping it back and forth. Where could a two-and-a-half-thousand-pound animal go that fast? Leaning out even more, I checked directly below to make sure the thing wasn't scaling the mast platform but couldn't find it.

I yelled at Matty, who was still standing at the railing of the bridge. "Did you see where it went?!"

Startled, his head jolted up at me. "What?"

"Get back in the bridge. Now!"

He waved. "I got through to the inland operations base!"

"Get inside!"

"Right, right!" He nodded and then began backing away. "They're sending a plane!"

"Get inside!"

He nodded again and I watched as he started to turn

toward the bridge. Drawing the scope to my eyes, I saw him as he hurried around and pulled open the door.

I was about to lower the scope when I noticed a shadow near the stairwell. Tracing the scope back across the railing where Matty had been, I couldn't see anything.

Seeing Matty exposed in that structure completely wrapped in glass, I had my worries that the bear had seen it too. It wasn't a good feeling to think we were on the monster's home turf.

I lowered the rifle and hoped the radioman had enough sense to stay put until I could get over there. Crossing back to the other side, I looked at the hole in the deck and thought about my friend down there, wounded and alone.

I circled the third floor and saw no sign of the bear, but that didn't mean he wasn't there. I started down the steps and thought about how after missing me in the hatch the first time, he'd silently waited until I'd approached before taking another shot at me.

Opening that door situated slightly above deck level was going to be interesting.

I reached the bottom and noticed part of a hatchway in the floor, covered by one of the crates. I could move it aside, but I was pretty sure the passage led to the main cargo area where the bear had set up camp before.

Sighing, I saw the door where I'd come in and once again wished I had a good 12 gauge with slug rounds—that, or a hand grenade.

I placed my head against the door to listen but didn't hear anything.

I reached out, slowly turned the wheel with one hand, and then looked at the latch and waited. I leaned the Rigby and axe against one of the crates and stepped back a bit, taking the Smith & Wesson out of my parka. I pulled the lever with one hand and pointed the .44 toward the door with the other, figuring six rounds were better than a single shot from the rifle.

All was quiet as I opened the door a little toward me before waiting another moment and swinging it halfway. I held the six-and-a-half-inch barrel toward the door, far enough away so that if the creature decided to swipe at me I wouldn't be standing there unarmed.

The light from the rising sun had lost its color and the outside world seemed flat and monochromatic. I pushed the door back a bit and paused in the short entryway, figuring there was no way the bear could do anything more than reach into the limited space.

I didn't check but was pretty sure the other direction was the same, and I pushed the door open farther, lodging myself in there but ready to retreat if I had to.

There was still no sound, and the only view I had was across the deck toward the port side.

I needed to get over to the hole I'd chopped in the deck and get word to Henry that our rescue was imminent, then backtrack to the bridge and get the whole story from Matty—all this without becoming an entrée.

I picked up the Rigby and looked at the masting axe, concluding that I was running out of hands. Stretching the strap, I pulled the .416 rifle over my shoulder and grabbed the massive hatchet, giving me a close-quarters weapon in each hand.

If I was going to get eaten, I wasn't going to go easily.

Stepping through the hatch, I checked down the small breezeway to the right at the steps leading to the main deck level. I pressed forward and scanned in both directions before stepping down onto the deck.

Turning in a full circle, I couldn't see any sign of the beast. Maybe he'd gone over the side, sensing that this much contact with human beings probably wasn't going to end well for him.

Now on deck, I continued walking and scanning before finally stopping at the hole. "Henry?"

"Yes."

I knelt, still checking in all directions. "Hear anything?"

"No."

"Me neither." I threw my voice into the darkness again. "Are you okay?"

"As well as can be expected."

"Matty got through to the inland base and there's a plane on the way. I'm going to get you out of there."

"That is reassuring."

"I've got to go see him and find out what's going on but then I'll be back."

"I am not going anywhere."

I stood again and circled, even going so far as to walk over to the railing and look down at the ice, which, to my surprise, wasn't there. In its place was lapping water where large chunks of ice had broken up and were now swirling in the current and floating away.

"This is not good . . ."

The voice from the deck rose up again to meet me. "What is not good?"

"The ice is melting, and the ship is breaking free as near as I can tell."

"And why is that not good?"

I walked back over, scanning the horizon, which had indeed changed, the topography of icy mounds having flattened out making it later than I wanted it to be. "If the inland operations base sends a rescue plane to these coordinates, it would be helpful if we were here." I glanced up at the bridge. "I'm not sure if Matty's aware of the situation, and I'd like him to find out our options."

"Please do."

I turned toward the hole. "I'm going to get you out of there."

"You said that already."

"I'm saying it again."

"Go."

"Right." I walked toward the bridge and scanned the deck but didn't see anything. Maybe the bear, feeling the ship beginning to dislodge itself, decided to seek greener pastures? At least I hoped that was the case.

Staying to the right, I crossed the deck toward the bridge, still keeping a wary eye out as I took the steps from the left side and climbed upward. Pausing before coming out on the upper deck, I leaned back, thinking I might've seen something.

I raised the Smith & Wesson and watched as a thin vapor of condensate drifted over the opening like a fleeing spirit.

Maybe it was the smoke from the stoves in the living quarters.

"Walt?"

I almost choked. "Matty?"

His head appeared in the opening. "I got through."

Slouching against the inside wall, I collapsed. "Did you not hear what I said about that bear being out here?"

"I know, but after that first time I saw him, I haven't seen him since." He squinted at the sun. "It's getting warmer and the ice is breaking up, we're going to have to get off this thing." He looked back at me. "I sent them these coordinates, and they aren't going to be able to land a rescue plane if we get swept out to sea. Besides that, this ghostship might just be setting sail for another decade-long loop into the Beaufort Gyre . . ."

"Meaning we could get lost out here for a while?"

"Yeah."

"I don't think we have the supplies, let alone the brandy for that."

"No."

I started to struggle to my feet. "All right, you get back in there and appraise the inland base of the situation, and I'll do the same for our friends in the living quarters."

"Sounds g—"

I turned, and he'd disappeared.

Laughing, I shook my head. "You don't have to go that fast."

There was no response.

"Matty?!" Raising the .44, I held the railing as I rushed up the stairs, keeping the big revolver in front of me before stopping dead in my tracks. Blood pooled at the edge of the top step, then dripped over the edge and ran down onto the next tread.

Lunging forward, I'd just gotten to the landing when something struck me, sending me flying backward and down the ice-covered stairs. I'd slid halfway and lay there trying to gather my wits when the bear's head filled the opening at the top of the steps, blood stringing from his jaws as he attempted to force his way into the opening.

Try as he might, his massive bulk wouldn't allow him to squeeze into the confined space of the covered stairwell. Mad with frustration, he lunged his misshapen, blood-covered head at me, his jaws snapping only inches from my boots. He opened his mouth in a silent roar—the only sound being the air rushing from his bellows-like lungs, spraying droplets of blood in its deathly silence.

12

I kicked away and slid farther down the steps, my hands scrambling behind me to feel for the Smith & Wesson as I lay with the high-powered rifle at my back.

The bear roared its silent bellow again, its huge head stretched out above and toward me where I could see that the damage to the side of the monster's muzzle stretched down and enveloped the left side of the creature's muscled, hairless throat where scar tissue massed.

Lowering its bloodstained head, it stared at me through the one eye, huffing and pressing against the inside walls of the stairwell that groaned with the pressure. I had to give credit to the Lindholmen shipyard in Sweden and the wrights who had constructed the contained stairwell as the bear pulled back a few inches and studied me with the glaring eye. We stayed like that for a long while, me unmoving and him unable to get at me. I could see the wheels turning in his giant head that blocked out what little light there was. The eye cast about in search of some way to pull the gangway cover apart, but seeing none, the beast thrust his head forward slowly, his quivering nostrils only a handsbreadth from my boot.

I lay unmoving in my inverted position, breathing heavily as I cleared my throat. "Look, why don't you just get off this boat and go hunt seals?"

His head inclined to one side, giving the single eye a better perspective as he continued to study me with his one ear tilted in my direction.

I felt something at my hip and slid a hand down behind my parka, where I could feel one of the hand flares that must've fallen from my pocket.

It was possible he'd never been this close to a human being he wasn't actively eating, and maybe the first time he'd ever heard one speak up close and personal. "I don't know how, but I'm going to get my friend out of here . . ."

The ear twitched again, but that was all.

"Even if it means killing you." I snatched the flare and yanked off the cap, watching as it struck to life, the red light filling the gangway revealing the details of the creature even more.

He pulled his head and the bulk of his body out of the makeshift tunnel before swiping a paw strong enough to graze his claws into my boot. I tried to draw my leg back, but the claws dug into the heavy rubber, and I could feel myself being inexorably dragged up the metal stairs.

I rolled onto my side, kicking at the beast, and threw the flare where I thought its face might be, then in desperation I searched the ground around me for another one to throw.

A great blast of fetid air burst out, but again no sound came from his damaged vocal cords as the beast pulled farther away from the stairwell. I felt the pistol under me and grabbed it, turning on the steps and grabbing the railing to leverage myself into a semi-standing position. My hip hurt like hell where I'd fallen, but I moved forward, keeping an eye all around the opening as I got to the top, where blood continued to pour over the steps and leaked down onto the next lower tread.

There was blood pooled in front of the opening as I leveled the .44 in all directions. There were also smears across the ice going around the bridge structure and toward the main stack.

I moved in that direction and could see where the creature must've attacked the radioman at the stairwell, killing him instantly, before coming back to see if it could also get me. As far as I knew, this was not normal behavior for any large carnivore.

The blood trail led past the stack and over the roof of the living quarters to the mooring gear at the stern and then, once again, disappeared.

The single lifeboat still hung from one set of chains, clanking in the breeze, but there was no sign of the bear or Matty.

"What the hell is going on?" I yanked my head to the side and looked down to where Roy was standing at the railing on the main deck, looking up at me. "We heard a lot of noise on the roof and thought something was happening?"

"Get back inside! Now!"

"What's going on?"

"Get inside—I'll be down in just a minute. Matty's dead and Henry's still trapped, so get inside and stay there. That bear is around . . ." I frantically surveyed the aft area where the blood smear stopped. "Somewhere."

The navigator spared no time doing as I said, and I waited until he closed the hatch below me before returning to the bridge. I opened the door and stepped inside, checking both ways before securing it behind me.

I moved through the doorway that led to the radio shack and could see the telegraph key along with a small wire-ring notepad and pencil in which Matty must've taken notes about the conversation with the inland operations base. Scribbled on the first line were the coordinate longitude and latitude of our rescue along with more numbers, which were probably the frequency they were using and a time.

3:20 p.m.

I flipped a switch and watched as the radio dial illuminated dimly.

I tapped on the telegraph key and listened but didn't hear

anything, when suddenly a furious rhythmic clicking began. I stared at the device, deeply regretting not continuing my radio studies in boot camp. If inland operations were trying to inform us of something, I wasn't the one to translate.

Figuring we'd have a better chance if I got Jerry, the copilot, in here to listen to the thing, I turned the device off to save the batteries and tucked the notepad in my inside pocket.

Slowly pushing the hatch open, I scanned the walkway, holstering the .44 and swinging the Rigby around to examine it. There was some superficial damage to the rifle from the fall on the stairs, but it appeared to be in good working order, and I carried it at the ready in case I encountered the bear somewhere on the deck.

Still seeing nothing, I took a step and slipped on the dark ice of the blood-soaked upper deck and then stood there staring at the freezing liquid.

How could it freeze so quickly?

I was lost in thought for a moment before concluding that if I didn't get going, none of this would matter. Swallowing, I took the stairwell down but went to the right and toward the living quarters where I knew some anxious people were waiting.

I pulled the door open and stepped into the warmth again, peeling off my goggles. I tipped my hat back as the others gathered. "Matty's dead."

Roy was the first to speak. "What happened?"

"That bear got him."

Marco was the next. "It's still out there?"

"Yep, and it doesn't appear to be going anywhere." I placed the rifle on the table along with the flares and pulled off my gloves, stretching my hands out to the nearest stove. "Henry's still trapped below, and he's seriously hurt. I was able to chop a hole in the deck and get the food and water to him, but we've got to figure some way of getting him out of there by 3:20."

Roy glanced at the others and then me. "Why 3:20?"

I took the notepad from my pocket, opened it, and pointed toward the sprawl of numbers. "Matty contacted that inland operations base and gave them the coordinates to where we are. That's when they said they'd be here. Now, assuming whatever they get here in is larger than the Polar Pig, they're not going to be able to land near the *Baychimo* and we're going to have to get to them."

Jerry whistled through his teeth. "Out on the ice."

"Yep." I pulled out my pocket watch and checked it. "That gives us about three hours, and then it's going to get very, very dark."

Blackjack sat at the other side of the stove. "But?"

"Yep, but . . . With the sun coming out the ice is shifting, and this ship could dislodge itself and be headed out to sea, where it'll be a lot harder for them to get us—if they can even find us."

"Why couldn't they find us even if this thing breaks free?"

"This ship has been appearing and disappearing for more than a half century. Matty had a theory there's a current that keeps sweeping up the *Baychimo* and circling her around every ten years—now I don't know about the rest of you, but I'd just as soon miss that cruise." I turned to Jerry. "How's your Morse code?"

He shrugged. "Rusty, at best."

Roy nodded. "Mine's better, but I did find this." He held out a small coin, tossing it to the copilot. "It's old, with the send-receive Morse code engraved in it."

"You're our guy, then." I pointed at the notepad again. "Here's what we've got, but when I tapped in some gibberish they came back with a flurry of responses. You're going to have to go up there and stay in contact with them until they get close."

He took the notepad. "Yeah, that would be pretty near to where we are, and it would take them every bit of that amount of time to outfit a plane and get it here."

"So, we're going to need you in the radio shack behind the bridge."

"What about that bear?"

"It's still out there." I turned to Blackjack. "Have you ever seen a bear act like this one?"

"No, but there are legends among my people that coincide with the cycle of the Beaufort Gyre." She shook her head as she sat there with the cub in her lap, stroking it as it snored. "Tales of the nanurluk, the great bear god who cannot be killed and who decides the success of hunters and punishes those who break his rules."

"Well, what's out there is no legend, just a highly developed ambush predator—and he enjoys it."

Marco's eyes darted toward the others and then back to me. "What do you mean 'he enjoys it'?"

"He killed Wormy and that sow polar bear and Mike, went after Henry and killed Matty . . . He's gone after me at least three times, and there's no reason for it as near as I can tell. He can't be attacking us for food. Even as big as he is there's no way he needs to eat that much."

Marco looked at me, incredulous. "So he's doing it for sport?"

"Can you think of anything else?"

Roy shook his head. "Territory?"

"No—Mike, Wormy, and the other polar were killed out on the ice, off the boat."

Marco clutched the lower part of his face in panic. "What rules could we have broken?"

"It doesn't matter." I noticed Blackjack placing the cub back on the table where she surrounded it with the gun cover and a few cushions. "What does matter is that that rescue plane will be here in less than three hours. We've got to get Henry out of the hold and ourselves out onto the ice where we can get picked up and get him medical attention."

"You can't be serious." I turned to Marco, who backed away. "We'll be lucky if any of us make it out onto the ice, and even if we do, what then?" He lifted a finger toward the hatchway. "That thing is just waiting for us to go out there, and you want to go on some kind of rescue mission?"

"The one thing I'm not going to do is leave Henry here to die."

"He's already dead, man." He gestured toward the door again. "That thing is out there and anybody who goes after him is dead too." Marco pointed to the group. "I'm right, and you people know it."

I faced the others, but none of them would look me in the eye.

Finally, Blackjack retrieved her rifle and came over to stand with me as Jerry started to speak.

The copilot paused for a moment and then shook his head. "You said yourself that he's badly hurt. I mean, what are we going to do, carry him out of here bleeding all over the place—that thing'll be on us in no time."

Roy glanced at me and then back to his crew member, adjusting his glasses. "It's not a vote. Besides, you'll be in the radio shack."

"I can't do that." Jerry raised his hands and then let them fall. "You're going to need two guys to get that big Indian back here."

We all turned to Marco, who backed against the wall. "No fucking way."

Jerry fished in his pocket and took out the coin Roy had given him, flipping it to Marco. "Relax, all you have to do is go up the back staircase to the radio shack and communicate with the incoming plane, the inland base, or anybody else you can get hold of."

Marco seemed pleased with the turn of events and then stuffed the coin in his pocket as Roy faced me. "Okay, so what's the plan?"

Sliding a chart to the side, I pulled the blueprints of the *Baychimo* from the pile of ledgers and charts on the table and laid them on top, placing a fingertip at midships. "This is where Henry is, near the tween-deck centerline bulkhead, and the only way to get him and then get him out is through the stairwells near the bridge castle, or up here through the cargo hatch covers. The problem with one of those is that I think as big as he is, the only place that bear can get into the cargo hold and back and forth between decks is the main cargo cover. Now, if we can get him forward and past the heavy-lift rig, then two of us can go below and get Henry out and back here."

Roy looked at me dubiously. "Then what?"

I sighed. "I'm not sure, but if we're all together it should be easier to figure something out."

"Like who to feed to the bear?"

I turned to Marco. "If you're not going to help that's fine, but if all you're going to do is make things more difficult, then I'm going to make some really quick decisions about that."

"There is only one problem with your plan."

I smiled wryly at Blackjack. "Only one?"

She nodded, hugging the big rifle close as if to warm it. "Someone has to be bait."

"You've got to be kidding."

I zipped up my immersion suit and buttoned my parka,

stuffing my pockets with hand flares. "I think Henry is right, it got burned down in one of the coal holds and it still remembers that—fire might be the only thing on the face of the earth it's afraid of. You should've seen it when I got the flare out and threw it at its face." I looked through the ice-covered portholes at the dying light as the ship shifted again. "The sun is going to be gone in about an hour and that bear has the advantage in the dark—it knows this place." I picked up the remaining flares and stuffed them and the flare gun in my parka pockets before making sure both the .44 and the .45 were in the inside pockets at my chest. "We're going to need some kind of diversion so that we can get to Henry."

"So, you're going to head to the forecastle and drink and sing sea chanteys until that thing shows up? Then what, offer him a round?"

Tossing my hat on the table, I opened the cabinet and grabbed the full bottle of Armagnac. "You never know." I gestured toward Blackjack, who stood by the hatchway door with her hand on the lever. "That's what she's for. If I can get her up in that mast platform and the cargo crane operators on the third floor where I was, she should have a clear view of the foredeck." Pulling the stopper off the bottle, I started to take a swig and then thought better of it, replacing the cork and lodging it fast with a pat from the palm of my glove, then tucking the bottle into my parka. "Maybe he won't be so quick with a few .416 slugs in him."

I moved toward the door and then turned back to the two

crew members standing near the table with Marco. "Are the two of you ready?"

They nodded their heads at each other but not with much enthusiasm. "When do we go below?"

"Not until you hear a lot of noise from the front. You can go up the back stairs to the radio shack from here without being in the open though. Just wait by the door on the bridge. When you hear all the noise, come out and go to your right and down the covered stairway and into the hold. Don't pay any attention to all the blood . . ."

Roy swallowed. "Right."

"Then head down one level to the second deck and take the gangway forward—Henry is in the second cargo hold on the left." I handed them four of the flares. "Take these, because it's dark as pitch down there."

Jerry stared at the blueprints like it was a deck of tarot cards. "Then what?"

"You get Henry and get the hell back up here the same way you went down."

He gestured toward where Blackjack stood. "Wouldn't it be faster to just take him around the left of the bridge on the main deck and bring him in this door here?"

"No. You'd be out in the open and, believe me, that is not a place you want to be."

Marco finally spoke. "What about me?"

"You stay in the bridge in that radio room; if they don't get a confirmation from us, they might give up the rescue attempt."

He nodded. "Right."

"And then just stay there, you're more likely to hear and see them from an elevated position when they fly in."

"Right."

I looked back at Roy and Jerry. "Don't fool around, when things start happening out there, they're going to happen quick, and I'd just as soon not end the day as bear chow. It should take me about five minutes to get in place and then I'll head forward." I pointed to the disassembled M16. "Does that thing work?"

Jerry sighed. "No."

"This plan . . ." Roy bit a lip. "How do you know he'll follow you?"

"He's had three shots at me so far . . ." I thought about it as I adjusted my hat. "I think it's gotten personal." I pulled the .44 from my parka and then buttoned it back up and stepped toward the door as I cocked the revolver.

Blackjack turned the lever and then pushed it open, the door slowly squealing like a stuck pig, the gray light spilling across the floor like an unwelcome invitation.

Moving slowly, I aimed the big revolver to the right and then to the left, having firsthand knowledge of the speed and reach of the beast.

There was no sound, which wasn't surprising, but I took the chance of looking over the rail above and below to check if he was out there on the walkway. I'd just started to step out when I glanced up. Seeing as how he was genetically programmed to reach down for his food, there was no reason why he couldn't be up there.

Leaning out over the rail, I was pretty sure that the next thing I was likely to see would be the gaping maw of the beast, but there was nothing there besides the slapping of icy waves against the hull slamming against the side of the ship like a multitude of hammers.

I motioned for Blackjack to follow me and then carefully made my way toward the front of the bridge and past the aft cargo hatchway. As I'd seen before, the cover was intact on this one, so the polar bear wasn't using it to get below, which meant we were relatively clear to the mast platform.

I turned and noticed Blackjack staying near the bridge but eyeing the scow that hung above our heads.

I spoke quietly. "Something?"

She joined me while keeping an eye out in all directions. "If this thing does break loose, it's possible we could get the lifeboat in the water and get back to the ice."

"Not likely with that current."

"Better than nothing." She shrugged. "I don't like the idea of being stuck on this ship with this bear for ten years."

"You and me both."

We were now in the open and halfway across the aft cargo area. "You really think this thing is some kind of bear god?"

"After hearing about the gyre, I wonder if it's not possible that some remnant sleuth DNA of primitive *Ursus maritimus tyrannus* possibly could have survived on it through the centuries?"

"Did you just use the term 'sleuth' of bears?"

Ignoring my question, she gazed into the middle distance.

"*Ursus maritimus tyrannus* was an extinct ancestor from the late Pleistocene epoch, a forerunner of the modern polar bear—and you must admit, he seems indestructible."

"Well, so am I." I studied her for a moment and then refocused, determined to keep my guard up. "When you get inside, head straight to the third level. The window's open up there and he can't get to you." She nodded and then followed me as I cut to the center of the ship and peered around the other side before pulling the lever, opening the door, and ushering her inside. I began closing the door behind her, but she placed a hand against the hatch, holding it open. "Don't get too confident."

I rummaged up a smile. "It's an animal."

She took a slow breath, blowing it out between her lips. "You are proud of this plan of yours, using yourself as bait?"

I didn't say anything.

"Has it not occurred to you that he has done the same thing, using your friend?" She continued to study me. "It is every bit as smart as you, and perhaps smarter—you have underestimated it while it has not underestimated you."

The door closed and I listened as she locked it tight and I glanced around, still seeing and hearing nothing.

13

It was another hundred feet to the cargo gear, but it felt like a thousand. Beyond that was another cargo cover and then the elevated area of the prow where I'd make my stand.

There were a few flaws in my crafty plan. First, there wasn't anywhere to go if it all went wrong, other than overboard into the freezing water and the sloshing ice thumping against the hull, which wasn't all that enticing. Second was the obstruction of the scow that hung overhead from large cargo cranes that stood between the bridge castle and the foredeck, which provided an enormous blind spot where Blackjack wouldn't be able to protect me from above.

As I moved forward, I could see the hole in the deck across

the cargo cover and circled back, going up that side so I could tell Henry what was going on.

Kneeling by the hole, I rested the big revolver on my knee and called down in a whisper. "You there?"

His voice echoed from the cargo hold. "Where else would I be?"

"How are you?"

"Not bad, I am not bleeding anymore." A moment passed. "Maybe I am out of blood."

"Yep, well help is on the way." Scanning the area, I asked another important question. "Have you seen our friend?"

I heard some rustling, and his voice grew closer. "He was outside the hatchway awhile ago, but I have not heard anything from him lately. Strange, in that he does not make noise."

"I don't think he can, whatever it was that burned him damaged his vocal cords. I honestly don't think he can make a sound."

He laughed weakly. "Which makes him that much more dangerous."

"Yep." I checked the deck around me again, determined not to be caught unaware as I had been before. "We've got a rescue plane coming in from the inland base at 3:20, but the coordinates are going to hell because the good steamship *Baychimo* has decided to break up the ice and set sail. We've got to get you and the rest of us off this thing toot sweet. The crew guys Roy and Jerry are going to be coming down to get you while Blackjack and I draw that big bastard away."

"And how, pray tell, are you going to do that?"

"I'm going forward and she's in the bridge castle with that .416 Rigby."

There was a pause. "That is a single shot weapon."

"Four plus one, she's got a whole box of ammo."

"That she has to load the breech in that bolt action one at a time."

"Look . . ." I growled into the hole in the deck. "This plan has enough holes in it, and I don't need you to poke any more, so unless you've got a better one?"

"I do."

I sighed. "I'm listening."

"Leave me."

I stared at the hole. "Not likely."

"Listen to me, Walt. I probably will not make it out of here—"

"Shut up."

"I do not even know if I can stand anymore."

"Shut up."

"Listen, there is no sense in endangering other lives by trying to get me out of here. All I am going to do is get more people killed." There was another pause. "Instead, I will drag myself through this hatchway down here and let that animal have me, providing all of you with enough of a distraction to get away."

"No."

"The choice is not yours."

"Yep, it is. Our plan is already underway and if you change

it now, you really will be putting people's lives in danger—what do you think will happen to Jerry and Roy when they come strolling down there?"

Another pause. "Course number two and three?"

"Exactly, now get yourself ready, and when they arrive you get the hell out and back up to the drawing room and the captain's quarters, got me?"

"Walt?"

"What?"

"Be careful, I do not think this is a normal animal."

"I'm getting that." Laboring up, I pulled out the .44 from my parka. "Be ready."

His voice rose from the hole in the deck, even weaker than before. "Roger that."

I looked up to see Blackjack taking position in one of the corner windows, the barrel of the big rifle aimed where I stood.

She nodded as I moved toward the railing to the left, keeping my back to the ocean and moving forward in the one section of the main deck that had no side, just railings.

Glancing over, I couldn't see anything other than the crumpled ice and, of all things, the bright blue Thiokol Cat. "What the hell?" I scanned the area but could only see prints where someone had climbed out of the buggy and approached from this side, possibly climbing onboard and scrambling onto the crumpled ice and onto the available section of the main deck, where I now stood repeating myself. "What the hell?"

My sniper watched me.

I looked down at the machine, the exhaust still steaming. "The Thiokol from the plane, it's down there on the ice!" I noticed the tracks where it had been driven beside the ship. "Somebody drove it here. I don't know who, but I'm sure glad to see it—gives us more of a chance than that damned scow, which we don't even know floats."

"You better hope it does."

I turned to see another individual leaning against the bridge castle in the shadows, holding another .44 on me. "Bergstrom?"

Moving forward, the dying sun struck the side of the Texan's face where a bandage was wrapped around his head underneath his ball cap. "How are you doing, Walt?"

"Not so great as of late, but I was feeling better after seeing the Cat and you . . . But now I'm starting to get a sinking feeling."

"Yeah, sorry about that." He gestured with his sidearm toward me. "You wanna throw that hand cannon onto the deck there?"

I did as he requested, watching it slide a few feet from me as I turned back to face him. "What's going on, Mike?"

"Change of plan, of course that's all this colossal polar fuckup has been from square one . . . Kind of like when that ice screw cracked me in the head. I was going to get you out there and get rid of you. I figured you were the only one that posed a real threat to us, but then I thought it was a good way of separating us so that I was free to do the dirty work.

I climbed in the Cat and stayed in there until the winds got so bad, then I just jacked it up and headed away from the wind, which kept me from going ass over teakettle last night."

In my peripheral I could see Blackjack leaning out from the window, aiming the big rifle down at the oil man. "I'll repeat, what's going on, Mike?"

He took a step forward, but not far enough for Blackjack to get a clear bead on him. "Are you a company man, Walt?"

"In what way?"

"Northstar really needs developmental access to this Arctic Refuge, ole buddy, and that means killing this proposition that Wormy was pushing."

"And that meant killing Wormy?"

"Well, that wasn't the plan, but I guess things change, and my associate saw an opportunity . . ."

"Marco."

Bergstrom made a face, rolling his blue eyes. "I guess things didn't go well out there on the ice."

"Henry checked his weapon and noticed there was a fourth round missing after the warning shots."

"Yeah, Marco's kind of impetuous. Anyway, I'm the one that's supposed to fix this little problem."

"You think killing Wormy is going to stop a federal proposition for an Arctic Refuge?"

He shrugged. "It's a start. Wormy was one of the biggest advocates in the National Science Foundation, and without

his USGS research they'll have to delay their counterpro-
posal, which should give the company time to jump in with
some of our political friends and grind this refuge thing to a
halt. So, my turn to repeat—are you a company man, Walt?"
Bergstrom took another step forward, closing the distance
between us and almost to where Blackjack could reach out
and touch him with a 400 grain hollow point that would
pierce even his black heart. "We could all be very rich if we
play our cards right."

I took a deep breath and blew it out, moving toward the
cargo hatchway to my left. "We?"

"Me, you, and Marco. That Indian buddy of yours . . . I
don't think we can let any of the others in on it—loose lips
sink ships, you know."

"So, we kill them?"

"Well, we don't have to. We can just hop in the Cat and
head back inland and let the SS *Baychimo* do our work for
us, you know what I mean?" He laughed. "I can't believe
Matty and you guys found this thing. Everybody's heard the
legend . . ." He nodded toward the cargo hold. "Is there really a million dollars' worth of furs down there?"

"Why don't you see for yourself?"

"And then what? Load it into the Cat? I don't think that's
gonna work—anyway this Northstar deal is gonna rake in a
hell of a lot more than that. So, what do you say? With you
on our side, there's nothing that can stop us . . ."

"Oh, I don't know about that."

"I was afraid you were gonna say that." Shaking his head, he took another step forward, focusing his aim on me. "I'm really disappointed in you, Walt."

"Well, you're not the first."

"This isn't going to end well."

"No, it's not." I took a step toward the railing. "Money, Bergstrom? Is that what this is all about—money?"

"A lot of money, Walt, a lot of money. Enough money that I can tell those executives at Northstar to kiss my ass. I've been in the oil business since I was twelve years old, floor hand, roustabout, roughneck—I've done it all. Hell, I've forgotten more about this business than those assholes will ever know. The kind of money we're talking about here will let me start my own empire, not to mention getting in on the expansion this kind of operation is going to call for." He studied me. "What are you smiling about?"

"Something I told Wormy. How money is power, and power is money and if you yank back the sheets at midnight you're going to find both of them in bed together."

"Too bad he didn't take your advice."

"You mind if I have a drink before you shoot me?"

"Sure, but don't try anything funny." I carefully unbuttoned and reached into my pocket, pulling the bottle of spirits from inside as he kept the muzzle of the .44 trained on my face. "What the hell is that?"

"French Armagnac, we found it in the captain's quarters." Pulling the cork, I took a quick swig, just enough to wash out my mouth and then held the bottle out to him. "Wanna try it?"

"I have to admit that you're taking all of this extraordinarily well." He took a step forward and reached out his hand. "Sure."

And that's when ballistic lightning struck.

I wasn't sure how someone as small as Blackjack could hold the heavy rifle with more than twice the recoil of a .30-06 so steady, but after the thunderous clap of fire, the brief echo of the bolt action speedily reloading another round was impressive.

Mike's screams screeched in the freezing air as he collapsed to one side and onto the deck, and I couldn't help but smile as he clutched his butt cheeks, both of them having been monumentally pierced by the big Rigby.

"You know, it would appear the Inuit have a remarkable sense of humor."

He continued screaming as he flopped around on the deck, still holding the Smith & Wesson.

I took a step toward him as he lifted the .44 toward me. "Who in the hell?!"

I nodded toward the tower. "Blackjack."

Staying on his side, I watched as he dragged himself over to the cargo hatchway and leaned against the metal side to keep her from getting another shot into him. "Call her off!"

I raised my hand toward the top floor of the castle bridge where Blackjack held her aim on him, to ward her off. She reluctantly did as I signaled. Walking back over to the railing, I picked up my .44 and looked down at the Cat. "How long do you suppose before that thing falls through the ice?"

He didn't say anything. I turned, and he wasn't there.

Gone.

I stared at the spot where he'd been lying on the deck, the smear of blood where he'd dragged himself over to the cargo hold. The pool of his blood already beginning to freeze into the gray wood.

I looked up at Blackjack and watched her head scan from side to side, her dark eyes darting around the deck. From the look of confusion on her face, I could tell she couldn't see him either.

I placed my hand to the side of my mouth, calling to her. "Where did he go!?"

She didn't answer but frantically surveyed the deck.

Walking over to where the blood continued to coagulate, I could see the smears where Bergstrom must've pushed himself up. But then where did he go? There was no more blood leading away, so the only thing he could've done was climb into the hold below.

I'd just taken a step in that direction when I heard the unsecured corner of the hatch cover, flapping in the breeze.

Why hadn't I noticed that before?

"Walt?" Henry's voice rose from the hole I'd cut into the main deck. "Walt."

"Yep, I'm here."

"I think you should know . . ."

I'd just turned toward the small hole when I saw some-thing move in the darkness of the corner underneath the cargo cover—only for an instant—and that was the last thing I remember seeing.

It was as if the ship had suddenly been turned over, the blast of movement and deathly silence bouncing me back against the railing and throwing me sideways, where I slid across the deck before crumpling into the steps of the fore-castle break.

I lay there for a moment, shaking my head and trying to regain my senses before rolling over to see the enormous bear crawling the rest of the way out of the hold. His fore-paws, merciless face, teeth, and throat were dripping with blood—an indication as to Mike's final fate.

He didn't hesitate as he gathered his incredible bulk onto the deck, the compressed force of his inconceivable muscle mass and agility on full display as he looked directly at me with the singular eye.

The .44 in my hand felt like a peashooter. If I was lucky, I might get one round off before he was on me, or I could stick to the original plan.

I dropped the revolver.

Lumbering into a sitting position, I slid onto the first step as the unbelievably gigantic creature began a soft pad in my direction on paws the size of serving trays, his grotesque, blood-covered head swaying in anticipation.

I lifted the bottle of Armagnac, making a brief toast and then pouring the rich, sharp-smelling liquid over my hat, hood, shoulders, and arms. Just for good measure, I lifted the vintage bottle and took a swig before slinging it at the bear, watching it burst on the wood of the main deck in front of him.

I'm pretty sure he paused not because of the action but because of the smell of something he wasn't used to, or worse yet, something that might echo in that great, cavernous skull of his, a primitive spark of something—something dangerous.

He huffed, but no sound emitted from his mouth, only the blood-drool and bits of flesh from Bergstrom's body.

I lifted the flare from my pocket and snatched off the cap, watching the red spark explode and leap to life like a living thing. Touching it to my sealskin parka, I watched as the flames raced across the surface of the thing, enveloping me as I stood and threw the flare at the puddle at the bear's feet.

With a dreadful *whoosh* it bloomed up from the hard deck and for the first time I saw that lone eye grow wide and wild as the giant reared and backed away.

Standing, I took out two more of the flares and struck them, holding them in each hand as I spread my arms in an attempt to make myself appear larger than I was. I wasn't as large as he was, but being covered in flames, I was the embodiment of the one thing that had done him damage.

I was a walking inferno—and I was coming for him.

He swiped at the deck in a bluff charge, then backed away as I advanced, walking among the licking flames on the deck as if they were a part of me.

I wasn't sure what happened to Blackjack; maybe her rifle

jammed, maybe she ran for help, but I couldn't see her in the open window of the castle bridge. It was possible that she was still there but with the limited view of my goggles and the fact that I was on fire, I couldn't see shit, except for the bear, which was as big as a proverbial barn.

I saw the eye shift as he actually thought of turning and running, but I couldn't have him diving back into the cargo hold to kill Henry and the two others.

I lunged at him with the flares in my hands and watched as he reared up on his hind legs in an attempt to make himself bigger—or maybe he was about to pounce.

In a last-ditch attempt, I reared back and threw both flares at him, and he did exactly as I'd hoped he wouldn't do, which was leap for the cargo hatchway. It made sense; this was his home and even though it was the place where he'd been almost burned to death, it had protected and nurtured him for all these years.

There was only one more thing I could do, so I charged toward him in an attempt to cut him off before he got there, the flames still undulating all over me. He reared back, preparing to strike at me, and all I could think was that at least I was going to die warm.

The clanking of the chains and the thundering of the heavy-lift rig above us made a thrashing and metallic sound as the large scow pivoted for only a second before crashing down on top of us.

I fell backward as the bear leapt for the cargo hatchway with incredible speed.

But not fast enough.

The weight of the open-water craft slammed down into him as he tried to get in the hatchway, catching him across his great back as the lifeboat exploded on the deck, the remains of it and the great bear half-falling into the cargo bay as I lay there propped up on my elbows watching the polar's leg hanging over the edge, unmoving.

14

I was trying to make sense of what just happened. I lay there on fire as Blackjack came from around the tower structure with a blanket. Throwing it over me, she beat on my body until I could feel that the flames were smothered, and I almost missed their warmth.

I mumbled from underneath the blanket. "What the hell just happened?"

After a moment, she pulled it back and smiled at me. "I thought we needed a change of plan."

"Boy howdy." Shifting a little, I sat up as she continued to pat out what flames were still attempting to flicker back to life and burn away my legs. "Are you all right?"

She laughed. "More importantly, are you?"

"I think so." I pulled the goggles from my face, only slightly singed from my efforts. "Did you just drop a boat on that bear?"

"I did." She sat on my leg and looked back at the torn cover of the cargo hatch. "The rifle jammed, and I thought it was the only way to stop him. Fortunately, the winches were mechanical and didn't require power to operate the release. So, yes, I dropped a boat on the nanurluk."

"God bear or no god bear, I'm glad you did."

She climbed off me and then pulled me up by one arm as I got my balance and looked around at the scattering of flames that remained, which gave every impression that they would be dead soon, the Armagnac no fair combatant with the Arctic wet and cold.

Spotting the hole where my friend lay, I stomped over and knelt. "Henry?"

There was no answer.

"Henry?" The next time I leaned down, shouting into the hole. "Henry!"

"I am right here."

I turned to see Roy and Jerry, half carrying the Cheyenne Nation from the direction of the bridge—I saw that they had wrapped him in one of the steerage blankets not unlike the one Blackjack used to put me out. Stumbling over to them, I felt a surge as the ship slipped just a bit, breaking free from the ice a little more. "How are you?"

His head rose, and I'd never seen him so pale. "Alive."

"C'mon, Bergstrom delivered the Thiokol down on the

ice but he's dead. I'll explain later, we've got to get off this ship before it breaks completely loose." Reaching out, I smothered another sprig of flame that had suddenly sprung up from my arm.

The Bear stared at me. "Excuse me, but are you on fire?"

"Only a little bit." I stood and steadied myself as Blackjack joined us. "Where's Marco?"

Roy seemed surprised by the question. "I don't know, I'd assume he's in the radio room where you told him to go."

I stooped down, meeting Henry's eyes with mine. "Can you make it to the Cat?"

"I can make it to Fairbanks if you point me the direction." He breathed deep. "You must get the bear cub from the stateroom."

"You've got to be kidding."

"No, she is the reason we are being allowed to escape."

I patted his shoulder, and he grimaced as I pulled my hand away, gesturing to the other three as I searched the surface of the deck. "Where's my gun?"

Blackjack handed me the .44 as I started toward the aft of the ship. "Get him off this thing and in the Thiokol; if the ice starts to break up, back the Cat away as far as you have to. If you don't see me in the next ten minutes, get the hell out of here and head to those coordinates Matty wrote down, southwest." I nodded at Roy. "Right?"

"Correct."

Henry attempted to pull away from them. "Walt . . ."

"Go. I've just got some quick business to take care of." I

crossed the next hatchway and got to the main stairwell that led to the bridge. I continued around the side of the bridge castle and opened the hatch of the warm room, stepping inside and going over to the table, where I ignored the malfunctioning M16 and scooped up the miniature bear, tucking the rifle cover around the squirming cub and turning to go.

"That's far enough." I looked up to find Marco standing at the stairwell to the bridge aiming his .357 at me. "You know, I ought to kill you for just hitting me, but instead I'll make you a deal—I don't shoot you and you don't shoot me."

I gestured with the pistol I had at my side. "I think I'll still shoot you, anyway."

He laughed, using his other hand to open the throat of his parka. "You can try, but the best you can hope for is a draw. Now why don't you place that .44 on the table here and then climb down there with your friends where you're needed and get off my boat."

"Your boat?" I stared at him. "You're staying on this thing?"

"Salvage. Law of the sea. We'll see how this all works out, but I've got some friends coming and I don't need all of you here cluttering things up." He gestured with the pistol. "So, why don't you just hand over the .44 and you people just get out of here and take your chances on the ice."

"You never made contact with the inland base, did you?"

"No, but who knows, maybe Matty did."

"Marco, this ship is slipping back into that spiral of the Beaufort Gyre, so if your friends don't get here quick, you're going to disappear into the ice and snow never to be heard from again."

"I'll take my chances now that you killed the bear. Besides, I know how greedy the people who are coming after me are, and believe you me, they'll find me."

"I wouldn't count on it."

He gestured with the revolver. "Put the gun on the table, I might still need it."

Stepping forward, I did as he said and watched as he took it and turned to the window where a small patch had thawed enough for a view outside. "You better go, that Thiokol is going to sink before long." When he turned back to me, I pulled the .45 from under my parka and pointed it at his head.

"Marco, the only reason I'm leaving is because I know that the fate you're facing is going to be more harrowing, colder, and excruciating than anything I can come up with—and I think Wormy and Matty would agree."

I carefully backed out and stomped across the deck around the holds to the forecastle break where the others were carefully loading Henry into the Thiokol and starting it up.

Giving one last look to the cargo area where the shattered scow had fallen and blown apart, crushing the bear, I shook my head and thought of the millions of dollars' worth of furs down below. It just wasn't worth it, and I couldn't see how anyone could convince themselves otherwise.

It was then that I saw it.

A slight flicker of movement from the giant bear's leg.

Just a tremor.

I kept watching, but it didn't move again, and I assumed it was a side effect of postmortem rigor or involuntary primary relaxation. Standing there holding the wrapped-up cub, I thought about going over and checking, but there wasn't time because the ship was beginning to float free.

I climbed over the rail with my precious bundle. I could see the larger portions of ice were breaking up and splitting as the *Baychimo* continued to completely dislodge itself. There was a section of slab ice that had upended, providing a ramp that led to a relatively flat area I hoped would hold my weight and the cub's. Hanging there by one hand, I slid on my side to the area below and was satisfied it wouldn't break even if my view was obscured by the piles of ice shooting up in angles all around me.

I didn't care for the noises the ice was making and ran toward the Thiokol, hoping to get there before the sea opened up and swallowed me whole. I slipped and fell but was still able to see the roof of the Cat and its aerial.

Scrambling over the ice, I could see where the sheet leveled out and the prints where the others had gone. Following those, I watched as the motor was gunned and the Cat rocked back and forth on the treads.

Moving a little faster, I got to the side and slammed a fist onto the door, which immediately opened, with Roy's hand coming out to hoist me up. "Boy, we were just about to get the hell out of here and leave you."

Climbing onto the treads, I handed him the bear cub and then swung in and took a seat, slamming the door shut. "How's Henry?"

Blackjack's voice rose from the back as she took the now squalling cub. "I . . . I don't think he's going to make it."

I looked at her and then at him lying on the floor. "I'll take that bet."

Jerry turned to me from across the console. "I got the inland base on the radio and assured them of the coordinates, but we've got to get there quick before it gets completely dark."

I pointed southwest. "Go."

"Where's Marco?"

As we pulled out, turning to the right and clearing the geometric monoliths of ice broken free by the ship and sloshing in the current like a miniature mountain range, I gestured back toward the *Baychimo*. "He decided to stay."

As the Thiokol trundled across the ice, I couldn't help but stare as I saw Marco standing at the railing watching us as we drove away, even going so far as to wave. "You stupid bastard."

I'd just started to turn away when I thought I saw something, a shadow—an incredible ursine mass lumbering up and towering right behind him in the enveloping mist. "Stop!"

Jerry ignored me, his gaze ahead as he handled the dual levers of the Cat, negotiating our way from the edge of the ice and water. "Can't, or we won't make it."

I pressed my face to the glass and looked at the *Baychimo*, aware that I might be the last living soul to ever glimpse it, trying to see Marco—but it was as if he'd never been there, and perhaps he wasn't.

He, the ship, or any living thing on it were never seen again.

EPILOGUE

"And I'm supposed to believe that story?"

I glanced up at him from the chessboard. "You're burning our steaks, old man."

Shaken loose, Lucian scrambled out on his one leg and slid the glass door open. He stepped out onto the patio of the Durant Home for Assisted Living's room 32, opening the grill and retrieving the meat before returning, leaving the door a crack open. He placed the three T-bones on the wooden cutting board and centered them on the table as we joined him, Henry placing the wrapped talisman beside his plate.

The Cheyenne Nation scooted in his chair as Lucian studied him. "So, I take it you died?"

My friend took a napkin from the table and unfolded it in his lap. "Numerous times."

The old sheriff turned to me. "So, they got you out of there?"

I settled myself in and I broke open my baked potato, loading it up with butter, sour cream, cheese, chives, and bits of bacon. "They did."

"And you never heard of this Marco or the ghostship, this SS *Baychimo*, again?"

"Nope, the last sighting was us back in '70. We filled out all the reports for the company, the Coast Guard, the FBI, and the Alaska State Police, but nothing ever came of it. They tracked Marco's citizenship back to Venezuela, but they never heard from anybody saying he survived or knew of his whereabouts."

Lucian picked up his fork. "That was a damn bit longer than ten years ago . . ."

I took a bite and chewed. "Yep."

"What happened to the cub?"

Henry smiled. "Martha was taken in by the Alaska Zoo in Anchorage, where she lived to be thirty-five years of age."

"What do you think happened to the *Baychimo*?"

I shrugged. "I'd say its luck ran out and it sank. Even as stout as it was, a ship like that can only withstand being crushed by the ice so many times before something has to give."

"Or perhaps not." We both looked at the Bear as he sawed off a portion of his steak and popped the bite into his mouth, chewing and then finally speaking again. "I prefer to think that she is still out there, somewhere, in her continual transit, afloat and drifting through those eternal Arctic mists— still retaining her mysteries, reluctant to ever give them up."

I smiled. "And the nanurluk?"

"He is there too, forever sailing the Beaufort Gyre through the Transpolar Drift, the primordial king of the northlands."

"Oh, horseshit." Lucian began eating in gusto, ignoring the Cheyenne Nation as the Bear sat there studying him before reaching down and unwrapping the small bundle to reveal a claw over five inches in length.

"Good lord . . ."

Slowly standing, the Bear began unbuttoning his shirt.

Lucian shot me a puzzled look and watched as Henry peeled the cloth over his broad shoulders and turned, revealing his heavily muscled back—where four shimmering grooves of scar tissue raked across the length at a diagonal like quadruple streaks of iridescent lightning.